The **CATE CARLISLE** Files

VIPER'S NEST

ISLA WHITCROFT

PICCADILLY PRESS • LONDON

For my first and dearly loved friend Joanna Sparks
(1964 – 1973). The happiest girl I ever knew.
Best friends forever!

First published in Great Britain in 2012
by Piccadilly Press Ltd,
5 Castle Road, London NW1 8PR
www.piccadillypress.co.uk

Text copyright © Isla Whitcroft, 2012

A catalogue record for this book is available
from the British Library

ISBN: 978 1 84812 243 7 (paperback)

1 3 5 7 9 10 8 6 4 2

Printed and bound by CPI Group (UK) Ltd, Croydon, CR0 4YY
Croydon, CR1 4PD
Cover design by Simon Davis
Cover illustration by Sue Hellard

PROLOGUE

The hot Mexican wind blew in angrily from the ocean, sweeping over the low valley, then up the mountain ranges and on to the inland rainforests.

By the time it reached the ancient ruins, the wind was almost at gale force – whipping through the surrounding jungle and howling round the towering pyramids and the crumbling stone shelters, up to where the vast stone warriors were standing proud, their flat, expressionless faces and smooth bodies glinting in the fractious moonlight as they had done for over a thousand years.

A large wooden hut stood a few metres away from the site, almost engulfed by the jungle on three sides, close to a small river which was usually placid and calm, but was currently a frenzy of foam and raging water. Inside the hut, lying on narrow bunk beds, four members of the University of California archaeological student team were trying hard to snatch some sleep.

But it wasn't just the raging wind that was keeping them

awake. There was another reason too. Each one of them was struggling to control their feelings of excitement, the realisation that, against all the odds, a bunch of students had cracked a conundrum that had eluded the finest brains in archaeology for the best part of one hundred years.

'You awake, sis?' A pale face framed by short, dark, curly hair appeared over the top bunk and peered down into the gloom below her. 'Sis?' she said more urgently and then, spotting the headphones wire, grinned to herself.

She picked up her pillow and, aiming carefully, threw it down to the bunk below, chuckling to herself as her twin sister sat up with a snort of annoyance.

'That'll teach you to ignore me,' Jade whispered, dodging as her twin retaliated with a pillow of her own. 'What's the point of having a twin if you can't talk to them in the middle of the night?'

There was silence for a few seconds and then the girl on the lower bunk whispered, 'What time do you think the professor will get here?'

'Dunno.' Her twin was uncharacteristically non-committal. 'But when she does arrive, once she's checked everything out, then we'll know for sure.' She tried hard to keep her excited voice low. 'Just think, this time tomorrow we could be in the papers all over the world. Famous! On TV, radio – maybe they'll even make a film about us. The four students who changed the history of the world. We'll be known as the Famous Four. With you the most famous of all. Better get yourself an agent!'

Amber giggled, then dropped her voice even further. 'Honestly, Jade, you do get carried away. But still, it is amazing. To see what I saw. The first people in what, over a thousand years? Incredible.'

'What are you guys rabbiting on about?' A Scandinavian

accent came floating through the thin plywood partition. 'Keep it down, huh? We all need to get at least a few hours' sleep.'

'Sorry, Stefan,' the girls said as one, then lay back down on their pillows.

'Try counting ancient treasures,' Jade whispered, making Amber smile in the darkness. 'Get in some practice for the real thing.'

But sleep still eluded Amber, her exhaustion not enough to quell the flurry of images in her head. She could see herself a few days earlier, out for an early morning stroll into the fringes of the jungle by the ruin. She had heard an outraged hiss and rattle, and she had known immediately what it was. Her heart had started thumping and she'd forced herself to remember the wildlife training she had sat through on her arrival at the site.

'Retreat quietly and gently,' Thor had told her. Although he was an archaeology student too, he was also a bit of a wildlife expert. 'Snakes are rarely aggressive unless they feel threatened.'

Amber had pushed herself sideways through the scrubby bush, retreating as quietly and quickly as she could from the deadly viper. Then, as she made her escape, her foot had slipped down into the ground. Her leg and suddenly half her body disappeared into a widening, crumbling hole that seemed to tunnel right back under the base of an ancient wall.

Forgetting the tropical rattlesnake, she had sprinted back to camp, grabbing a couple of torches and a startled Stefan, and within minutes the pair were through the hole and into a damp tunnel, marvelling as it opened into a wide stone passageway.

As the light from their torches played on the stone walls, they saw them – ancient wall daubings, the colours still clear and rich, telling stories of the artists and their daily lives. The scenes were filled with hunting, sailing and children playing.

As always when she saw such drawings for the first time, Amber found tears clouding her eyes. Even in the midst of the grind of ancient daily life – the hunger, the disease, the murderous rituals – someone had still found time to create art.

'Awesome,' Stefan had breathed. He was by far the most experienced of the team, already on his doctorate in ancient Mexican history and the only one of them qualified to lead a dig. 'Well done, Amber. A-grades all round, huh? These are as clear as any on this entire site.' He moved the torchlight systematically from one end of the wall to another. 'These ones look different though . . .'

Stefan and Amber moved towards some other paintings – small sketches, little more than stick drawings. Wordlessly, they examined them in minute detail. There was no mistaking their message. The story they were telling was mind-blowing, earth-changing – almost too much to take in.

Stefan straightened up and looked at Amber, and for a few seconds their eyes locked together in shock, recognition and amazement.

'I'll call the professor,' said Stefan flatly. 'She needs to see these as soon as possible.'

Amber nodded. 'I can hardly believe what I'm seeing. Do you think they're for real? Can they *really* be suggesting what they seem to be?'

Stefan shrugged, but his green eyes were wide, his face pale in the torchlight. He looked, thought Amber, as shocked as she felt.

'I can't see why or how they would be fakes,' he said, 'but we'll have to leave that up to the prof. But either way, we – or rather you, Amber – have found something really special.'

The CATE
CARLISLE
Files

Isla Whitcroft is a journalist who writes for national newspapers including the *Daily Mail*, the *Mail on Sunday* and *The Times*. She lives in Northamptonshire with her husband and three children.

But Amber wasn't listening any more. Something about the sketches wasn't quite right – something in the composition, the dynamics of the artwork was bothering her.

Amber dropped to her knees, bringing the torch close up to the warriors. That was it! The arrows, already unleashed into the air, were all pointing, not at the enemy and their snake-headed sailing ships, but to another invisible target. Trance-like, she followed their trajectory, tracing it over the cold wall with her fingers, oblivious to the icy water that was dripping on to her head from the stone-cold roof above.

Then she understood. The perspective was different to the usual style of artwork. The arrows were pointing *out* of the painting and away to the other side of the passageway. They were a message – a signpost.

Stefan was looking over her shoulder now and she heard him take a deep breath. He had spotted it too and his torch swung round in the direction that the arrows were pointing. The beam fell on what looked like the entrance to a tunnel in the wall.

But now their luck was running out. Not far inside the opening, stones and debris blocked the entrance, if that's what it was, completely.

For a few seconds the two of them stood there in silence, playing their torches up and down in a vain search for a way through.

'It's no good. We'll have to go back and get help. It's probably a dead end anyway,' Amber said, remembering other false and blocked trails that she had already experienced in her time here. 'Or if anything was there, it was probably looted years ago. Like most of the stuff around here.'

'Look at this, Ambs!' The excitement in Stefan's voice made

her jump. 'Up here – look! There's a gap. It's tiny, but it's there.'

Stefan shone his torch through the hole and stood still for what seemed like an eternity.

Finally he turned towards Amber and his entire face was lit up by a smile that was triumphant, awed, humble and thrilled.

'It's all here, Amber. It's here. Just like the painting showed us – and more!'

As they walked back out of the tunnel and into the fresh air, Amber had been too overcome to speak. But Stefan was already back in practical mode, taking charge of the situation.

'We can't breathe a word of this to anyone,' he said gravely. 'Not to the guards and certainly not to any of the tourists. We have to wait until the prof arrives to take over.' Stefan stopped and turned to Amber, who gazed back at him, trying to take in what he was saying. 'This has to be managed properly, by the ancient history experts, maybe even the Mexican government. Certainly not by us. I've got some experience, but this is way out of my league.' He gave a wry smile. 'They send four students to work on a very standard dig, not expecting them to find anything at all. And then this!'

Above them, the morning sun was already throwing out heat strong enough to make the grass they were walking through warm to the touch.

'Actually, Amber, I think it's best we just keep it between us four,' he went on. 'Don't tell anyone else, not family, not friends. The fewer people know about this the better. Agreed?'

Amber nodded, still too dumbstruck to speak. Stefan was right. If word got out about their find, the place would be swamped – media, tourists and dealers would be all over the site in hours.

But it was hard, so hard, to keep quiet about something as stupendous as this, particularly when Stefan told her it would take a few days for the professor to fly over from a remote dig in Ethiopia. It was only natural that she sneaked back there once or twice over the next few days. And completely natural too, to make a map of the cave and the blocked entrance. Unable to resist rummaging around the debris, she found a precious stone and what looked like an ancient dagger, which she took away and hid safely in the hut. After all, it was human nature to want to ensure that the world knew it was she, Amber, who had been the person who unearthed this amazing hoard.

Thank God she could at least share her excitement with Jade. That was the brilliant thing about having a twin. Amber could tell Jade absolutely anything and know it would never, ever, go any further.

The hut was nearly silent now. There was only the sound of gentle breathing and sleepy grunts as Amber's companions finally succumbed to sleep. Soon even Amber was drifting off, exhaustion finally getting the better of excitement, her final thoughts of the precious package lying just below her.

So no one stirred as the four men, their faces obscured by ancient death masks, their bodies shrouded in black, crept out of the tunnels which scored the interior of the pyramids and made their way carefully down the worn stone steps and across the main site.

They didn't hear the quickly subdued shout as two security guards and their dogs were overpowered. Nor, thanks to howling wind, did they hear the gunshots as the intruders showed the guards no mercy.

It was only when they awoke, starting with terror to see the demonic faces looming over them and the feel of cold shotguns at their necks, did they understand that they were at the beginning of a nightmare.

CHAPTER 1

Sitting at a vast window, perched high above Los Angeles International Airport, Cate Carlisle watched spellbound as yet another glinting metal giant powered down on to the baking-hot tarmac, swaying and rocking as it landed, before thrusting forward along the runway in a seemingly unstoppable surge.

As the red-white-and-blue jumbo finally pulled to a halt, Cate put her fruit cocktail down on the table, sat back in the white leather cocoon seat and sighed. The Encounter restaurant was stunning – with lava lamps on the bar, beaten metal covering the walls and a stupendous three-hundred-and-sixty-degree view – but this certainly wasn't how she had imagined she would spend the first day of her Easter holiday in LA.

It was whilst Cate had been waiting for her suitcases to appear on the luggage carousel that her phone had rung.

'Sorry, darling.' Her mother was, as usual, abrupt and to the point. 'Burt and I have been on a business trip to Mexico and it's taken longer than we thought to drive back to LA. Queues at the border.'

'Hang on, Mum,' Cate shouted, a hand over one ear to try to cut out the hubbub of the hundreds of passengers milling around her. 'Who's Burt, and where are you again?'

'Burt? Burt Tyler – he's my new partner, darling,' her mother said, sounding surprised that Cate didn't know already. 'And we're in Mexico. We've got a deal going with the locals to buy some gorgeous stuff. Sorry, darling, got to go. Go and grab a bite to eat and we'll pick you up as soon as we can. Can't wait to see you – and Burt is dying to meet you too.'

Then she was gone, leaving Cate silently fuming as she struggled to lift her two leather suitcases from the carousel. Driving from Mexico? Surely that would take most of the day. This was so typical of her mother. She hadn't seen her in well over a year and now she couldn't even make it to the airport to pick her up on time. She was so disappointed too; she had spent the last few hours of the journey psyching herself up to greet her mum and now . . . well, now it was all just a huge anti-climax.

Cate yanked grumpily at the smaller of the cases, half dragged it over the edge of the carousel and dropped it neatly on to her sandal-clad toes. Pulling a face and biting her lip to stop herself from yelling out, she managed to lever it on to her trolley and turned back to the carousel and reached for the other one. As she was hauling it off, her phone rang again and she struggled to balance the case and answer at the same time, only to drop that case too, as the call rang off.

'Here, let me help.' A large, tanned arm came over Cate's shoulder and pulled easily at the heavy case before placing it carefully on the trolley. She looked up in surprise and then further up again to see a very tall, tousled-haired boy, eighteen or nineteen, wearing a faded green UCLA Football T-shirt and grinning down at her.

'I thought you girls were supposed to be good at multi-tasking,' he said, in an unmistakable Californian drawl. 'You know, talking on the phone and lifting luggage at the same time. What happened to you?'

Cate's mouth dropped open. For a few seconds she didn't know whether to be annoyed or laugh at his cheek, but the amused glint in his brown eyes won her over.

She smiled back at him. 'I've been clumsy all day – I managed to drop my dinner into the lap of the snoring bloke sitting next to me when I was trying to change the film. He was pretty mad, but not because of the mess. My dinner was lamb cutlets and apparently he was a vegetarian. But at least it stopped the snoring.'

'Aha,' laughed the boy. 'A beautiful Brit. With a British sense of humour. Welcome to LA.'

He stuck out a large hand and shook hers enthusiastically. 'The name's Ritchie, by the way. Ritchie Daner. Second-year med student at UCLA and all-round knight in shining armour.'

'Cate – Cate Carlisle,' said Cate. 'Studying for A-levels at a school in London. Not normally a damsel in distress. Anyway, thanks for the help with the bags and, er, maybe see you around.'

'Where you headed, Cate?' Ritchie asked. Easily six foot four, he towered over her by nearly a foot, but somehow Cate felt reassured rather than intimidated by his size.

'Actually,' she began, 'I'm not quite sure. Well, that is, I'm going to have something to eat while I wait for my lift. My mum's supposed to be picking me up, but she's been delayed for a few hours.'

She flushed with embarrassment, more for her mother than for herself. She was under no illusions about how unreliable her mother could be, but she really hated other people to know about it. Even when, all those years ago, her mother had suddenly upped and left Cate and her younger brother Arthur at their home in London to 'find herself' in LA, Cate had not been able to bring herself to talk to her friends at school about what had happened.

Ritchie was fiddling around with his iPhone. 'I knew I recognised your name!' he exclaimed suddenly. 'I was trying to remember where I'd heard it before. You're that English friend of the twins. They told me you were coming to LA for a trip. And I've seen you on Facebook, on their pages too. Look, here you are.'

Cate stared at him blankly and then down at the tiny screen to see herself tagged in a grainy picture with smiling identical twins.

'You know,' he continued, almost jigging up and down with excitement, 'the twins? Amber and Jade. Curly dark hair, always talk at the same time. Didn't you hook up with them somewhere in Australia this winter?'

This time Cate's mouth did drop open. The Californian twins, wacky, funny and friendly, had been working at a turtle sanctuary with Cate and they had indeed stayed in touch through email and Facebook since then. In fact, a few days before she left London, Cate had messaged Amber to tell her that she was on her way and asking if the three of them could meet up.

'I've known the twins for years.' Ritchie laughed as he put his phone back in his pocket. 'Same school in West Hollywood and now we're at UCLA together. They're on an archaeological dig somewhere in Mexico but they're due back in town pretty soon. They said they were hoping to see you before you flew home. Just wait till I tell them I've seen you. Small world, huh?'

Cate grinned back at him. 'Amazing!'

He paused. 'Hey, do you want me to stay with you, keep you

company, till your mom arrives? I'm in no hurry.'

Cate was sorely tempted to take Ritchie up on his offer, but then pride – and exhaustion – got the better of her. 'No, it's fine,' she said stiffly. 'I'll just get something to eat, and wait for my mum. I'm pretty used to travelling on my own, I've been doing it for years, so you really don't have to worry about me. But hey, thanks, Ritchie. Maybe another time.'

'OK,' said Ritchie. 'But take my phone number and when you get to your mom's, if you're at a loose end, give me a call. I can show you around, take you to a few parties maybe? I'm only up in West Hollywood. I'd be happy to help out if needed.'

Cate had already decided she was going to wait for her mother in the Encounter Restaurant. She'd been struck by its space-age look every time she passed through LA airport and had always wanted to see inside.

It was odd to think that Ritchie knew the twins. The summer before, Cate had been offered a dream job on a yacht moored in the south of France. This job had dragged her into a hotbed of criminal activity and she was drawn into working as an investigator for IMIA – the International Maritime Investigation Agency – a shadowy group of investigators who never appeared on government lists, seemed answerable only to themselves and who were called in as a last resort to solve complex crimes all over the world. At the Australian turtle sanctuary, Cate found herself working for IMIA again – unbeknownst to her colleagues there, including the twins. IMIA considered her the perfect undercover agent because, as a sixteen-year-old girl, she could go places where men would almost certainly raise suspicions.

Cate had just finished her seafood salad when her phone rang. 'Mum,' she said eagerly, 'are you nearly here?'

'Sorry, darling.' The signal was poor, her mother's voice crackly and sharp. 'Burt's just got a call from a supplier. He's been offered some stock at a rock-bottom price and it's just too good an opportunity to miss, so we've got to make a detour. We'll be with you tomorrow now, not today.'

Speechless, Cate sat back in her chair, a toxic mix of hurt and anger beginning to churn in her stomach. Why oh why was nothing ever straightforward with her mother?

'Look, darling . . .' Her mother was using her placatory tone. '. . . Book yourself into a hotel at the airport and we'll be with you as soon as we can. I know your father always makes sure you have plenty of money in your account for emergencies when you're travelling, so you can pay by debit card and I'll reimburse you.'

Cate finally found her voice. 'Mum, I'm only in LA for fourteen days. I don't want to spend one of them in a smelly old airport hotel while I wait for you to get back from wherever you are.' She could hear her voice rising. 'I've come all this way to be with you. Can't you just leave Burt and get back to me now?'

Her mother tutted sympathetically. 'Calm down, darling. I know it's a shame, but it's only for a few hours really.' Her voice sharpened. 'Darling, I have to go now. Call me when you know where you're staying and we'll see you tomorrow.'

Cate slammed her phone on to the table and stared back out of the window. She wasn't sure whether she wanted to burst into tears or kick her suitcases out of sheer frustration. Instead she picked up a beer mat and crumpled it viciously into a tiny, unrecognisable ball.

'Something wrong?'

Cate started. She hadn't noticed the petite Asian woman who was sitting just to the left of her. How long had she been there? she wondered.

'Oh nothing,' Cate muttered awkwardly. 'Just that my lift is going to be late. About twenty-four hours late.'

'I heard you talking about needing a hotel.'

The woman was dressed casually in slim jeans and a beige top, but there was something about her businesslike attitude that Cate warmed to. Cate usually hated telling other people her problems, but right now she needed to talk.

'My mum was meant to pick me up but she has got delayed until the morning. So I'll have to spend the night in some vile airport hotel. I've been in grey old London for months and I'm desperate for a bit of surf and sun. I want to see the beach and the people and visit a cool coffee shop.' She stopped, aware that she was bordering on ranting. 'Well . . . you know what I mean.'

The woman looked thoughtful. 'As it happens,' she said slowly, 'I know somewhere that pretty much fits the bill. Have you ever been to Santa Monica?'

Cate nodded. She had always loved the vibrancy of that part of LA – the street artists, the surfers, the beautiful people chilling out.

'There's a great hotel there, right on the sand, just south of Venice Beach. The Erin. I often go there for coffee and I know people who've stayed. It's got a rooftop pool and apparently the bedrooms are incredibly cool. *Much* better than the airport hotels.'

'Sound amazing,' said Cate. 'Just perfect, but a bit above my budget, I expect.'

The woman rummaged in her neat black handbag. Cate noted the distinctive Chanel logo on the clasp. 'I'm sure I've got their card in here.' She pulled out a business card and waved it at Cate. 'Tell you what, why don't I call them for you? They know me there and I might be able to get you a good rate.'

'Wow,' said Cate, cheering up. 'That's really kind. Are you sure you don't mind?'

The woman smiled and picked up her phone. 'You go and order us both another drink and I'll make that call.'

CHAPTER 2

Sitting in the back of a cab as it crawled slowly down Santa Monica Boulevard towards the ocean, Cate could hardly contain her excitement. The huge Hispanic cabbie who had chatted about his seven children all the way from the airport along the snarled-up three-lane Lincoln Boulevard, had mercifully fallen silent, leaving Cate free to enjoy her first glimpses of the Pacific Ocean.

She could see it now, glinting beyond the low-lying brightly painted buildings that stood between the highway and the wide beach.

Cate edged forward in her seat, desperate to get to the hotel, change out of her jeans and T-shirt and hit the beach.

The cab indicated and turned left along Ocean Avenue, slowing almost to a halt as the driver looked out for the Erin Hotel. Cate wound down the window and sniffed the air, smiling with pleasure as she felt the sea breeze on her face.

No two buildings were the same: some were domed, some had chalet-style roofs, others were simply square concrete boxes painted in a variety of burned reds, bright blues and vibrant oranges. There were endless bars and restaurants, shops selling artwork, photographs, tattoos and books, and tiny cafés spilling out on to the hot concrete pavement. Where the sand met the sidewalk, Cate could see a wave of people running and power-walking along a wide tarmac path which edged the golden beach and stretched away out of sight behind the buildings.

'Ocean Front Walk,' said the cabbie helpfully, spotting her enraptured face in his mirror. 'The place where all the beautiful people come to be seen. The best place for people-watching in the whole of this crazy city.'

Cate grinned back at him before sending her mother a quick text to tell her that she was staying at the Erin Hotel by Santa Monica Pier. Hopefully it would save her mum a wasted journey out to the airport.

As the cabbie pulled to a halt, three girls in short skirts and vest tops swished past them, their rollerblades grinding on the pavement, long bare legs swaying.

'It's been a warm few weeks for April,' said the cabbie, watching the girls admiringly as he pulled the cases from the boot of his car. 'The forecast is good too. Have a great vacation now.'

Cate took the cases from him, paid him and turned towards the hotel. Pistachio-green with a pointed roof and balconies at every window, it wouldn't have looked out of place in an Alpine resort. But there the similarity ended. Rather than snow, sand edged the building and a bright yellow lifeguard jeep was parked outside the large porch, which trailed pink, red and yellow bougainvillea and ivy.

As Cate watched, two muscled surfers carried their brightly painted boards into the reception, pausing only to shake the sand from their beach shoes as they went in.

Bleached wooden floorboards and limed timbers gave the

reception area an unmistakable beachside vibe and, at the far end of the vast room, a small coffee lounge spilled out through large glass doors on to a wide balcony overlooking the beach.

She sent a silent thank you to the woman who had sent her there. Just after she got Cate a massive reduction on the usual room rate, she'd gone off to the ladies and didn't come back. She hadn't said goodbye and Cate felt bad she hadn't been able to thank her properly. Still, thought Cate, whoever she was, she had done her a huge favour. Talk about good luck.

Unable to resist, Cate headed straight for the view. The balcony was a suntrap; sand blown up from the beach was scattered over orange oversized beanbags and lumped up in hot silver mounds underneath her feet. Cate bent down and slipped off her sandals and leaned against the round metal railings to gaze down at the bright blue ocean, feeling her body unwind and relax from the effects of a long, hard British winter.

'Cate? Oh my God, is that you?' The booming voice came from behind her and made her jump. 'What on earth are you doing here?'

It was Ritchie, standing beside her, as large – if not larger – than he had seemed earlier in the day.

Cate flushed. 'My mum isn't coming until tomorrow now.' She found herself looking at her feet. 'So I booked myself in here for the night. Someone at the airport recommended it.'

'I'm so glad they did! My uncle owns this place. That's what I was doing here. Just popping in to see him. And now you. Seems like we're destined to meet!'

'Spooky,' she agreed. Suddenly she felt a wave of tiredness wash over her. 'It's great to see you again, Ritchie,' said Cate, 'but I really need to get up to my room and chill out a bit.'

'No problem. I understand. It's been a long day for all of us.'

He paused. 'Look, a bunch of us are having a beach party tonight. Nothing fancy, just a barbecue, some music, maybe a bit of surfing if the water isn't too cold. Join us if you want.'

Cate hesitated. Ritchie seemed like a nice guy, but she didn't want him to get the wrong idea. She was still hurting badly from her split with her French boyfriend Michel. She had met Michel last summer in Antibes, and it was he who had invited her out to Australia. But after he found out that Cate had spent the entire holiday working undercover for IMIA – and had been forced to spy on him and his friends at the sanctuary – he had decided to finish their relationship.

'I'm sorry, Cate,' he had said to her. 'I understand why you lied to me but I need honesty in my relationships. I guess I'm not sure how I can trust you any more – and I can't be with someone I can't trust. Not even as friends.'

Cate had tried to reason with him of course, to explain that her life – and probably the life of everyone at the sanctuary – had depended on her silence. But his mind had been made up, his face hard, so different from the affectionate, laid-back Michel she knew and loved.

'Hey, penny for them?' Ritchie was looking concerned. 'You seem really down. I'm asking you to a party, not a wake. No strings, just a fun few hours with nice people. It looks like you could use it.'

Cate pulled herself together and smiled. 'Sorry, Ritchie, you're right. I should get out there and enjoy myself. I'm only in LA for two weeks. Where's the party?'

'Past the pier – towards Venice. Meet you in reception at eight-thirty and we'll walk down together, if that's OK with you?'

'Thanks,' Cate said. 'I'm looking forward to it already.'

* * *

As Cate pushed open the door of her hotel room, her eyes widened in amazement. Opposite her, taking up an entire wall, was a huge mural of a giant wave breaking on to a beach where a young blond surfer was standing with his board at the ready. Thick sheepskin rugs dyed and cut into the shape of surfboards and camper vans were scattered liberally across the cool marble floor, and the bed frame was definitely made from bleached driftwood. Above it, battered surfboards hung at crazy angles from the ceiling and, just in case you missed the point, the lamp stand was a bronze cast of an arching dolphin.

The room was crammed with the latest gadgets and Cate broke into a grin as she took in a large, bright yellow Smeg fridge, a massive blender next to a huge bowl of fruit, and an iPod docking station on the granite work surface. Below the massive LED TV screen on the wall opposite her bed, the shelves were stacked with CDs and DVDs. Then, to her utter disbelief, Cate spotted a twin mixing desk next to a sound editing desk. The whole room was unashamedly, proudly beach chic and it made Cate want to laugh out loud. She really wished that her best friend Louisa and younger brother Arthur could be here to share it with her. It was just the most amazing hotel room ever.

Cate found the kettle and, while she waited for it to boil, unpacked a few of her clothes. She was here for at least a day and she decided to make herself feel at home. She chose a fennel tea from the variety of herbal tea bags in the small kitchen, walked to the window, pulled back the light muslin curtains and stepped out on to the balcony.

Cate eased herself into the blue wicker chair and gazed out at the ocean, revelling in the feel of the warm breeze on her face and bare arms. It was hard to believe that just twenty-four hours earlier she had been saying goodbye to her stepmother, Monique, at Heathrow Airport in the cold, driving rain of a grey April day. As she rubbed in some suncream, she wondered if it was too early to Skype Louisa and decided that it probably was. Instead, she shut her eyes and dozed, feeling the exhaustion of the long flight melting away.

An hour later, she was standing under the power shower, trying to decide what to do next. Half of her wanted to get into her beach stuff and go down to the ocean, lie on the sand and chill out. But Cate had been sitting down for a long time – she needed some exercise.

Cate headed back into the room and felt around in the bottom of her suitcase for her running shoes, pulled them out and threw them on to the bed along with her lycra shorts, T-shirt and cap.

As she pulled her thick, dark-blond hair back into a ponytail, her phone chimed with a text. It was from her mum, and was studded with a large amount of exclamation marks and smiley faces.

Amazing you're in Santa Monica! We have our new antiques shop there on Brendan Street. Mexicano Magic!! Will be back tomorrow evening and will pick you up from Erin. PS hope your father's paying!!! Xxx

Cate's jaw dropped. Her mother had a shop? She had always told Cate and Arthur how she hated to be tied down to routine, how the drudgery of a nine-to-five life would destroy her soul. This she had to see. Was it within running distance of the Erin? she wondered as she headed downstairs to the lobby.

'Do you happen to know where Brendan Street is?' Cate asked the receptionist, who had been chatting animatedly to a pair of lifeguards. She was black, with bleached-blond hair, four piercings in each ear and a very low-cut top. 'I'd quite like to run there if it's possible.'

All three turned slowly to look at Cate, then the receptionist smiled. 'I'll find it for you, honey,' she said, getting out a local map and beckoning to Cate. 'Yeah, here it is.' Her bright red fingernails pointed to a road a few kilometres south of the hotel. 'Brendan Street. Head along the beach towards Venice and then turn inland at Rose Avenue. Take this map with you and you'll find it, no problem.'

'Cool,' said Cate, turning to go. 'Should take me about an hour.'

'Mmm,' said one of the lifeguards, putting down the bottle of Diet Coke he had been swigging from and looking Cate up and down 'Do you know Santa Monica at all?'

'Sort of,' said Cate. 'Been here a few years ago.'

'Then you'll know to stay this side of the Pacific Highway,' one of the lifeguards called over his shoulder. 'You do that, you'll be safe.'

Cate thanked him. She was well able to look after herself. When her mother had left home, her father, a UN peace negotiator, had insisted she and Arthur join him in his world of diplomatic travel. She had travelled all over the globe and had found herself in many a tricky situation before her father had insisted they settled in London once Cate had started working towards exams. She also had a brown belt in martial arts, which gave her confidence. But it always made sense to listen to good advice.

She was just heading for the door when she spotted Ritchie. He was facing her, talking to a man, whose grey-streaked hair and the set of his broad shoulders seemed, weirdly, familiar.

She hesitated. She didn't want to interrupt Ritchie, but equally she would be mortified if he thought she was ignoring him.

Ritchie saw her and solved her dilemma. He beckoned her over with a friendly gesture. 'Hey, Cate, I was just telling my uncle about you. Come and say hello.'

The older man turned to greet her with a broad smile and, as Cate automatically put out her hand to shake his, she felt a shock of recognition. There, standing right in front of her, his lightly tanned face creased into a devastatingly handsome smile, brown eyes crinkling at the edges, was none other than Johnny James, possibly the most famous star Hollywood had produced in the last twenty years!

Charming, debonair, eternally single yet always seen out with the most beautiful girls, Johnny James had, almost overnight, risen from being a bit-part actor in a cult medical TV drama to one of the most accomplished and sought-after film stars in Hollywood. Just about every film he starred in was a box office hit, and year after year he was voted the number-one heart-throb by women around the world. And now, this . . . this god was standing in front of her, smiling his famous lopsided smile.

For a few seconds Cate thought her knees might just give out, but instead she managed to pull herself together and shake his manicured hand.

'Cate – meet Johnny James, aka my Uncle Jack.' Ritchie was grinning down at her, amused by her reaction. 'Uncle Jack, this is Cate Carlisle, a great friend of the twins.'

'Cate.' His voice was like liquid chocolate. 'So good to meet you. I hope the hotel has lived up to your expectations. How's the room?'

'Fantastic, thanks,' said Cate, trying hard to sound as if she was perfectly used to chatting to world-famous film stars. 'The view is amazing and I really love the mixing desk.'

Both men laughed.

'I'll let you into a secret, Cate,' said the film star. 'The desks were a bit of an indulgence of mine. I've always fancied being a top DJ and I thought if I put them in my hotel I would get round to using them.' He gave Ritchie a jovial nudge.

'Are you off for a run?' asked Ritchie, changing the subject.

'Best way I know to work off jet lag,' Cate said, smiling at him. 'Otherwise there's no way I'll stay awake for your party tonight.'

'I'm impressed,' said Ritchie. 'Enjoy yourself.'

Cate went round the corner of the hotel, out of sight, and then jumped up and down on the spot for a good twenty seconds at the same time as trying hard not to scream. She, Cate Carlisle, had just met *Johnny James*. *The* Johnny James! And they had actually shaken hands! Santa Monica was amazing. This was going to be the best holiday ever!

She punched the air, then reached for her phone and began to text Louisa. This her best friend had to hear.

CHAPTER 3

It was a few minutes before Cate felt composed enough to cross the sandy road at the back of the hotel on to the hot, dusty boardwalk to begin her run.

The boardwalk was packed. The baby buggies that Cate had seen earlier were gone, replaced by more serious joggers making a big show of drinking water and checking their bulky watches. Some of the men were shirtless, their tanned biceps bulging as they pounded along. The women were sporting the skimpiest of sportswear, perfectly cut to show off their toned arms and tight enough to make their washboard stomachs clear.

Cate thought she had never seen so much human physical perfection in one place. She glanced down at her pallid arms – she had a bit of catching up to do.

As Cate began to run, she could feel the energy surging back into her body. She could hear music and smelled the aroma of freshly ground coffee wafting from the beachside cafés. The smell reminded Cate of her summer holiday in Antibes in the South of France, when she had been working on the yacht belonging to the supermodel Nancy Kyle.

The boardwalk swerved inland through a leafy park then back out to the beach, passing a large sign for the Santa Monica Surf School. Cate felt like pinching herself. This really was the stuff of a hundred American TV dramas, from *Baywatch* to *90210*. She wouldn't have been in the least bit surprised if Angelina and Brad had suddenly popped up jogging alongside her.

South of Santa Monica, the crowds began to thin out and Cate pushed herself into a sprint, revelling in the feeling.

Then she spotted a sign for Rose Avenue. As she turned up the road, she passed a trio of buskers – a bass guitarist, a trumpeter and a sax player. Beside them, a couple of black guys were making the most of the driving funk rhythms, breakdancing and body-popping as the appreciative crowd whistled and clapped.

For a few seconds, Cate felt the now-familiar pain crunching her stomach. Michel played the saxophone and loved busking in the streets of his hometown, Antibes. He would have so enjoyed this. She shook her head, trying hard to rid herself of the image of his handsome face.

Cate realised she had now crossed into a more urban, grittier part of town. Huge art deco buildings rubbed shoulders with low-rise concrete cubes, a few luxury glass apartments jostled for position with clothes shops and internet cafés. A backpackers' hostel sported a huge ocean mural, a wine shop was heavily barred, and graffiti was everywhere. A group of down-and-outs slumped in a doorway shouted out to Cate as she passed.

But despite its edginess, there were unmistakable signs that this was still a highly desirable area. She turned down 7th, one of the wide avenues which bisected Rose Avenue, and all about her large brick buildings nestled next to modernistic glass-and-steel apartment blocks, their balconies all facing towards the ocean.

Cate saw tennis courts, expensive convertible cars parked in gated driveways and, here and there, the unmistakable blue turquoise flash of a private swimming pool.

She consulted the map. 7th led straight to Brendan Street via what looked like a small alleyway. Idly, she wondered about her mother's shop. What kind of Mexican antiques did she mean? Cate would bet a year's allowance that her mum's boyfriend did most of the work.

The alleyway was dark, the high walls covered with graffiti, the air oppressive and still. It was with some relief that she finally reached the end and headed back out into the light. Just as she did so, she spotted a road sign. Brendan Street. She had made it!

She looked around with interest. In between the houses, several garages and outbuildings had been converted into studios and small shops. Cate spotted an art studio, a vintage clothes shop and an ironwork forge, their brightly painted doors and windows adding to the arty, almost bohemian feel of the street.

A scattering of cars were parked on the pavement – a couple of gleaming sedans, and a dark-blue pick-up truck with enormous bull bars which stood opposite an old van with a spray paint portrait of a mermaid on the side.

Cate slowed almost to a walk as she searched for her mother's shop. She was concentrating so hard that she nearly fell over the legs of a man who was slumped on the pavement, his back leaning against an iron fence. His tatty jeans, holed at both knees, and his filthy hands gave him away as homeless and, as he sat still, eyes shut under the rim of a grubby white fedora, Cate thought for a terrifying moment that he might be dead.

Then he opened his eyes and gazed at her with startling clarity. 'Hey, watch it,' he said in a not-unfriendly voice. 'I was just having a doze.'

'Sorry,' apologised Cate. 'I wasn't looking where I was going.'

The man looked her up and down. 'Got any money you can spare?' he asked in a conversational manner. 'Or a cigarette maybe?'

'Sorry,' repeated Cate. 'I don't smoke.' She put her hand into her pocket and brought out a five-dollar note. 'That's for waking you up,' she said, grinning, and laid it down on the ground beside him.

Unlike many of her school friends, Cate didn't find homeless people intimidating. She'd helped out in a soup kitchen in London last winter and, talking to them, she'd realised that all it took was a run of bad luck for your life to fall apart.

'I'm looking for a shop called Mexicano Magic,' she explained. 'Do you know where it is?'

The man took the money and put it into a backpack that was lying next to him.

'Down there.' He pointed to the end of the street and squinted up at her. 'Watch your back.'

Cate looked at him questioningly, but he had already closed his eyes again. She shrugged and set off in the direction he had indicated.

She was almost at the end of the street when she spotted the shop, set back from the road on a dusty concrete patch between two tall apartment blocks.

Mexicano Magic was barely more than a shack, low-lying with a flat concrete roof and timber frames holding up dirty, white, concrete walls. The door, which sported a large *Closed* sign, was made of thick wooden planks and had obviously once been painted a jaunty orange. Now the paintwork was peeling and the old-fashioned lock rusty. Next to the door, a single barred window added to the grimy feel.

Cate stared at it with a mixture of curiosity and disappointment, and then immediately berated herself for being such a snob. Hadn't her mother said it was a new business? They were probably ploughing their money into buying stock – and in any case, there were signs that someone was making an effort. The sign above the door was freshly painted and colourful, and the small lawn which edged the shop was neatly mowed.

Cate was dying to see what her mother was selling. She had always loved the history and culture of the Incas and the Toltecs, ancient tribes that had built amazing temples and elegant towns, invented complex languages and used sophisticated medicine at roughly the same time as the Northern Europeans were wearing animal furs and living in mud huts. It would be amazing, thought Cate, if her mother was actually selling original South American artefacts. Maybe some tiny stone statues of long-forgotten gods, perhaps some beaded jewellery. But then, Cate supposed, if she was doing that, she wouldn't be dealing out of a small concrete shack in the backstreets of Santa Monica. No, it was a nice dream, but the reality was that her mother's shop would probably be repro city. But hey, thought Cate, everyone had to start somewhere.

Cate was about to text her mother and tell her she had found the shop when her eye caught a movement from inside the building. She moved closer to the window and stared through the dirty panes. There was no light on inside but she could definitely see something – or someone – moving around at the back of the room.

Cate wandered up to the orange door and tried the handle. It was locked so she rapped loudly and waited. There was no reply. Only the parrots cawing from the pine trees above her and the cicadas rasping from their clumped grasses disturbed the silence.

Puzzled, she looked through the window again, but this time she couldn't see anything. Maybe she had imagined it, she thought, or seen a reflection. Reluctant to leave so soon, she went up the small pathway that led around to the back of the shack to a narrow strip of tatty garden, which ran back fifty metres from the building.

Litter lay everywhere – dirty rags, old cardboard boxes and wooden crates that had been piled into a precarious mountain against the back wall. An open fridge had been dumped against the fence next to the wreck of a motorbike.

At the end of the garden stood what looked like a concrete bunker. Just a few metres of the building was above ground and, at the front, steps led down. It reminded Cate of the old bomb shelter a friend of hers had in his back garden in London. Today, Cate's friend used it as a sleepover den and rehearsal room for his band, the thick concrete walls proving the perfect soundproof barrier, keeping his parents and the neighbours happy.

Suddenly Cate felt, rather than saw, a movement behind her. She wheeled round to see a man carrying a wooden crate emerging from the shop. For a few seconds the two of them stared at each other before he let out a bellow.

'Whaddya doing? Get outta here.'

Shocked at his vehemence, Cate stood her ground. 'What are *you* doing here?' she countered. 'This is my mum's shop. Does she know you're here?'

The man walked menacingly towards her. 'I'll tell you one more time, lady,' he said, quieter this time, his Latin American accent sharp and distinctive, 'you get outta here or you'll be sorry.'

Cate knew that the sensible option would be to back away, leave him to whatever he was up to, maybe call her mother once she was at a safe distance from the shop. But she couldn't help herself. Looking at his narrow eyes flickering nervously, it was obvious he was up to no good. Was he stealing something from her mother's business? She felt a surge of adrenalin and clenched her fists, noting his flabby stomach and puffy face. He wouldn't be expecting an attack and, she thought, he probably wouldn't put up much of a fight.

She took a step towards him. 'Put that box down.' She was surprised at how angry she sounded even to her own ears. 'It doesn't belong to you.'

To her surprise he did just that, laying it carefully on the paving slabs that edged the back of the shop. But Cate's relief was short-lived. As he stood up, Cate saw his eyes dart over her right shoulder. She spun round and found herself face to face with a small man who barely came up to her shoulders, but who, to her horror, was carrying a baseball bat.

Trapped between the two men, Cate made a split-second decision. She launched herself towards the little man, kicking the bat and flicking it up and over the fence behind him. For a few seconds he stood silent, rooted in shock. It was long enough for Cate to grab his still-outstretched hand and spin it around and behind him, forcing his arm high up his back. He was helpless in her determined grip.

'Don't take me on,' she barked at the taller man who was staring at her with disbelief on his face. 'Not unless your friend here wants a broken arm.'

He nodded wordlessly.

'Now sit down, right there.'

He did as she said, lowering himself stiffly on to the grubby paving stones.

'Missy,' the man found his voice, 'this is a big mistake. We're allowed to be here, I promise you. We're just helping a friend out, shifting stuff.'

'So why the baseball bat, huh?' Cate asked tersely.

Cate tightened her grip on the man in front of her, who shuffled uncomfortably but stayed silent.

'We've been given a key and were told to collect some boxes from this place,' his colleague continued. 'We get a lotta trouble in this job. Thieves, bandidos, druggies. They rob our van and threaten us. Maybe my friend here thought you were stealing from me. He don't talk English good.' His sweaty face took on a pleading expression. 'Come on now, missy, we don't want no trouble. Just let my friend go, we'll get on with our job.'

Cate looked at them speculatively. In their cheap, shiny tracksuits, with sweat pouring down their faces and their hands shaking, she had to admit they looked harmless enough. Perhaps they were helping Burt out after all? But on the other hand, they seemed very jumpy – too jumpy.

'We're just shifting stuff from over the border,' the man repeated stubbornly. 'Doing a job. You understand?'

Her anger subsiding, Cate shrugged. She wasn't going to push it any further, not now. It would be best to get out of there, then call the police, she decided. They could sort this one out.

As she walked away, she took her phone out. A flock of parrots screeched upwards and across the sky, shattering the silence and distracting her for a few crucial seconds so she didn't hear the footsteps that were coming up fast behind her.

Her stomach lurched as she felt something hard and cold being jabbed into her back and a low menacing voice hissed in her ear. 'Drop the phone, kid, or you're dead. Drop it.'

* * *

33

The air inside the bunker was damp and cold, cutting through Cate's thin T-shirt and giving her goose pimples. The smooth walls were just two metres high, the ceiling a slab of endless grey, giving the place the feel of a prison cell.

The three men were standing at the top of the short flight of stairs, out of Cate's sight, arguing furiously in Spanish. Cate listened intently, trying hard to work out what they were saying. She could speak European Spanish fluently, but Latin American Spanish was a little different.

'She didn't see nothing, boss, I promise,' the first man whined. 'She called out just a minute before you came. She saw nothing.'

'How do you know that? I only just got here, and you two *estupidos* don't know how long she might have been there watching you, maybe checking out the boxes when you were inside.' That flat, unemotional drawl again. 'And if she has, if she's seen what's in those boxes, then the whole operation is blown. Finished. And all of us with it.'

The other two were silent now.

'We take her with us,' the man continued, sounding almost pensive. 'We kill her and dump her somewhere up in the hills. She got a good look at you both, remember. We can't risk anything going wrong, especially not now.'

'No!' one of the other men shouted. 'We don't want no killing. We were paid to deliver those boxes, not to kill. Brother . . .' He was pleading now, desperate. 'Brother, I only just got out of that hellhole of a jail – I don't want to go back there.'

Cate could hear her heart thumping so loudly she thought the men must be able to hear it too. She looked frantically around her for an escape route, or something she could use as a weapon to defend herself. There was only a pile of wooden crates, stamped with Spanish instructions, piled up in one corner. Cate shuddered. But one thing was certain. She wasn't going to go down without a fight.

'She's just a kid. I can't kill kids. Especially not a girl. Look, man, we lock her here and go, OK? She'll be there a day, maybe two, maybe three. Who cares? A few days will calm the vixen down. By then we'll be back over the border, long gone.'

'Yes, he's right.' The other man was almost gabbling now. 'Come on, shut the door, leave her.'

The man, who was obviously their boss, snorted. 'You Mexicanos,' he sneered. 'No balls. Not like us Columbians. We show no mercy.' He paused. 'Still, it might be less trouble. OK, this time I'll listen to you. But any more screw-ups and it won't just be that kid who is lucky to be alive.'

They threw a bottle of water down the steps and slammed the heavy door. Cate heard the sound of a bolt being drawn across it. There was total blackness and a silence so profound it was almost suffocating. Her hands out in front of her, she shuffled in the direction of the stairs, sat down on the bottom step and tried to think clearly.

She was alive – that was the main thing. But she was trapped in a country where few people would miss her and, even if they did, how would they know where to start looking for her?

She wondered what had happened to her phone. Had the thugs retrieved it from the long grass where she had surreptitiously pushed it with her foot before she was marched to the bunker? She had to hope not. Her phone locator provided the best chance she had of being tracked down and found. In the meantime, she had no option but to wait it out.

She carried out a meticulous search of the bunker, feeling every inch of the wall from top to bottom with her fingers, pulling at bits of loose concrete in case they were the opening to a vent or a tunnel, banging on the ceiling until her knuckles were sore, but all to no avail.

Cate sat back down on the stairway. She was cold and the dampness was seeping into her bones and making her shiver. Every so often, she ran on the spot to try to get some blood moving to her frozen extremities.

The silence was beginning to bother her too. She started to sing her favourite Black Noir songs and that cheered her up for a while. Cate fingered the water bottle longingly. She was already thirsty but she was going to have to ration it. The question was how much and for how long? She could be here for days. She couldn't allow herself to think that she would be stuck here for ever.

Cate hated giving way to self-pity, but even so she couldn't help herself. She was entombed, alone in utter darkness.

CHAPTER 4

According to the light on her watch, two hours had passed before Cate heard a sound coming from above her. It was so faint that at first she thought she was mistaken, but then she heard it again – the low, muted thud of footsteps moving back and forth across the roof.

She raced towards the stairs, bashing her knee on a wall in her haste to get there. Ignoring the pain, she hauled herself up to the iron door and banged on it with all her might.

'Hello?' she yelled as loudly as she possibly could. 'Help! I'm in here.' She stopped and listened, then shouted out again at the top of her voice. 'In the bunker. I'm locked in. Open the door, please. Please!'

She heard the sound of the bolt being drawn and suddenly sunlight was streaming in, cutting through the darkness like a laser, making her eyes sting. Cate put her sunglasses on and bolted out into the daylight, gratefully gulping down lungfuls of fresh air.

It was the homeless man she had disturbed earlier, wearing a very bemused expression on his filthy face. His hair was long and greasy, his T-shirt covered with stains, but at that moment, Cate thought he was possibly the most beautiful human she had ever seen.

'Thank you,' said Cate, resisting the urge to throw her arms around him. 'Thank you a million times.' She paused. 'How did you know I was here?'

'You didn't come back out,' he said, eyeing her warily. 'I saw you go in but only those guys came out.'

He squinted at her. 'You OK?'

Cate nodded. 'I am now. I can't thank you enough.'

She put her hand out to his and after some hesitation he took it. His hand felt dry and old, although he couldn't have been more than forty.

'I'm Cate – Cate Carlisle,' she said.

'Jake Lomas.' He said the name slowly as if he had almost forgotten it. 'I sleep around here. I see all the comings and goings. No one sees me but I see them.'

A bell was sounding in Cate's head. Something Jake had said to her when she had given him the money.

'You warned me,' she said suddenly. 'You told me to watch my back. What did you mean, Jake?'

He turned away. 'I gotta go,' he mumbled, heading back up the garden.

'Hey, Jake,' Cate called softly. 'Please tell me. What do you know? What have you seen?'

But the tramp was gone, moving surprisingly fast for someone who seemed so disconnected from life.

Cate shook her head. She had other things to worry about now. She dropped to her knees in the long grass and began to hunt for her phone, praying that the thugs hadn't picked it up and taken it with them. But eventually she found it, lying near a discarded sandwich wrapper.

She picked it up thankfully, wiped it down, and dialled nine-one-one. 'Police, please,' she said. She took a deep breath. 'I want to report the illegal imprisonment of a sixteen-year-old girl.'

By the time the police dropped Cate back at the hotel, she was utterly exhausted. They had been polite but persistent, asking her to tell her story over and over again. The two policemen had been diligent at first, walking around the property, and checking for signs of a break in. They had knocked on neighbouring doors to ask for witnesses – but no one appeared to have seen anything. To add to Cate's intense frustration and annoyance, even the boxes and crates that had been stacked up against the shop wall had gone, with not even a trace of them remaining.

'I was locked in that bunker,' she explained for what must have been the seventh time. 'I walked in on something – I don't know, maybe a burglary? There were two Mexicans and a Columbian I didn't get a look at. They even talked about killing me. Here.' Using some tissue to hold it, she handed the female officer the water bottle. 'They gave me this. There may be fingerprints on it, DNA.'

The policewoman looked at her blankly as she ushered her into the police car.

They had driven in silence to the police station in downtown Santa Monica and Cate sat in the waiting area while a police sergeant shuffled files around a dirty Formica desk.

'We didn't find no sign of a break-in,' she said finally, looking over at Cate. The sergeant was as wide as she was short, thick glasses slipping down her podgy nose. 'We've only got your word for it that you were locked in that bunker.' She pushed her glasses back up her nose and gave Cate a stern look. 'We've made a note of your statement, but I'll tell you something for nothing. My shift only started two hours ago and we've already got one suspected homicide, three muggings and a hold-up in a pharmacy in broad daylight. So unless you can come up with a witness or, better still, some evidence that an actual crime was committed, then believe me, kid, we've got more important things to do than chase around after shadows.'

Cate took a deep breath. Losing her temper was tempting, but it wouldn't help. 'What about Jake Lomas?' She was determined not to give up without a fight. 'The homeless guy who set me free. Talk to him. He'll tell you.'

The sergeant glared at Cate. 'I've known Jake for years. He wouldn't know the truth from a lie if it hit him square between the eyes.

Cate shook her head slowly. She could see that it was pointless to waste time arguing. She wasn't going to get any further here. In any case, she was desperate to get out of this shabby police station and back to her hotel to shower off the stale smell of the bunker from her body.

She turned to go, but the sergeant wasn't quite finished with her. 'As you're a minor, we should really call social services and have you put into care until a significant adult arrives to collect you.' Her chins wobbled triumphantly, her eyes glistening with pleasure at Cate's horror-struck expression. 'But you got lucky. My boss is overwhelmed with paperwork and isn't too keen to take on any more tonight. So, instead, we're giving you a lift back to your hotel – and if you want to pursue this any further, call a lawyer.' She nodded towards the exit sign. 'Your lift is waiting, Cinderella.'

* * *

'Hey.' The hotel receptionist had an anxious look on her face. 'I'm glad you're back. I was just about to call the cops.'

If it hadn't have been so tragic it would have been funny, thought Cate.

'It's OK,' she said wearily. 'I just got a bit waylaid. But thanks anyway.' She headed for the stairs then paused. 'If you see Ritchie Daner, can you tell him I won't be up for the party tonight. Tell him . . .' She searched for an excuse. 'Tell him the jet lag won out in the end.'

Back in her room, Cate ran a huge bath, switched on the Jacuzzi setting and lay in the whirling bubbles, staring up at the ocean mural on the ceiling, enviously eyeing the pretty, tanned girls hanging out with fit boys at the water's edge. All Cate wanted was to be like one of those girls – carefree, normal, just enjoying a chilled-out holiday and some uncomplicated fun. Yet wherever she went things happened to her. Did she give off some vibe that attracted trouble?

On the other hand, she mused, as the water slowly cooled and the bubbles began to disappear, part of the reason she had loved following her father around the world was that they were always in the thick of the action, whether it was riots in Iran, civil war in the Balkans, or talking to wily tribal leaders in Afghanistan.

She cast her mind back over the last few hours. The cops were right: there had been no sign of a break-in. In that case, perhaps the men *had* been given a key after all. The question was by whom? There was no way they were acting within the law, so what were they up to?

Already the fear of being trapped in the bunker had faded, replaced by a burning desire to investigate why it had happened.

As she got out of the bath and into a luxuriously soft robe, she switched on the TV to the local news station. It was anchored by a heavily groomed couple who looked as if they had been carefully ironed before they came on air. To Cate, used as she was to the rather formal British news bulletins, their ebullient chat and flirty smiles seemed almost indecent.

'Ohhh . . .' The woman was talking now, her unnaturally bright teeth practically glowing in the studio lights. '. . . This is a piece of news I've been desperate to share with you all here at LATV. The gorgeous British supermodel Nancy Kyle has just arrived in town to make final preparations for the catwalk and fashion extravaganza at the Superbowl, a week Saturday. The gig is in aid of the charity the Mexican Street Kids Foundation, and Ms Kyle recently told LATV that she was organising the fashion show to coincide with the launch of a documentary into the plight of the street children, made by her rock-star boyfriend Lucas Black of Black Noir. Naturally Mr Black is headlining the music gig that will round off the evening.'

The picture on the screen cut from the studio to a shot of Nancy Kyle wearing a close-fitting purple evening dress on a red carpet. Camera lights were flashing and barriers were holding back cheering, waving crowds behind her.

'When Lucas first showed me the documentary I was heartbroken.' Nancy's Essex accent rose clearly above the hubbub of the red-carpet photographers and the cheers of the crowd. 'I sobbed my heart out, I really did. To think that just across the border from LA, one of the richest cities in the world, thousands of Mexican kids are sleeping rough every day of the year, living off what food they can find in the street and what money they can beg. They live in drains, sewers, on the edge of rubbish tips. Some are forced into slavery to get a roof over their heads, others resort to sniffing solvents and taking drugs just to get them through the hellish days and nights.'

Nancy looked soulfully at the camera, her green eyes huge and pleading. 'I've got five kids of my own and the mother in me wanted to rush down to Mexico and adopt all those street children. But I can't, so the least I can do is use what skills I have to help them in any way I can.'

She brightened. 'Loads of amazing designers have dropped everything to come to the show, and my really good friends Kate, Naomi and Aggy are flying out to model the clothes, and all my closest celebrity friends have bought tickets . . .'

As Nancy continued to describe the show, Cate turned the sound down and reached for her phone. Nancy was in LA! It would be brilliant to see her if the supermodel could spare the time. Since she had worked on Nancy's yacht last summer, Cate had stayed in touch with her, and had met up with her and her boyfriend, the Black Noir singer Lucas Black, in Australia. He'd helped her out big time, coming to the rescue when she most needed it.

Am in LA 4 hols + just heard u r in town. Would love to see u. Cate xxx

Cate had just pressed the send button when there was a rap at the door.

She peered through the spyhole and was surprised to see Ritchie. The receptionist must have forgotten to tell him about her change of heart and he had turned up looking for her. Cate was surprised at how pleased she felt as she let him in.

'Cate.' Ritchie's voice was subdued, his face pale. His earlier enthusiasm seemed to have vanished.

'You OK?' Cate asked, puzzled, as he strode into her room and grabbed the TV remote control, flicking through the channels until he reached CNN.

'Look at this. I've just seen it on the TV screen downstairs.' His voice was suddenly tense.

Cate followed his gaze. They were watching film footage of

43

what was clearly some sort of ancient archaeological site. The soaring steps of vast pyramids and the flat faces of huge stone warriors standing like giant watchtowers on the summit of the crumbling buildings were distinctive.

'That looks like Mexico,' Cate said.

'It is,' replied Ritchie tersely, still not taking his eyes from the TV. 'I think it's the site Amber and Jade have been working on.'

'Breaking news from Mexico,' intoned the voiceover. 'Four students have not been seen for two days after vanishing from an archaeological dig. Mexican police are refusing to speculate on the cause of their disappearance, or release names of the students, the site and any details of their university or nationality. Locals say the students may be from the United States. The US Embassy in Mexico City is refusing to confirm or deny this and the Mexican authorities are applying for a news blackout on the story. We'll bring you more as any further details are released.'

The bulletin came to an end. The news moved on to a bomb blast in Libya.

Cate and Ritchie stared at one another.

'Ritchie, there must be literally dozens of archaeological sites in Mexico and hundreds of students working on them from all over the world. The chances of Amber and Jade being the students in this story are pretty low,' Cate said eventually.

Ritchie clearly wasn't listening to her. He was fiddling around on his phone. 'Look here,' he said. 'Neither of them have updated their Facebook page in the last few days. And Jade is always on Facebook, at least twice a day.' He shook his head. 'I don't like this. I've just got a bad feeling.' He looked at Cate, his eyes anxious. 'Me and the twins, we go back a long, long way and I really care about them. They're like sisters to me. I even persuaded Uncle Jack to sponsor their time at the dig. I couldn't bear it if anything had happened to them. I'm calling their mom to find out.'

He punched a number into his phone and wandered out on to the balcony. Cate heard him talking in a quiet murmur, his voice sounding grave and subdued. A knot began to form in her stomach, a ball of worry that seemed to grow by the second.

She thought back to how welcoming the twins had been when she had first arrived at the turtle sanctuary in Australia. She'd loved their positive, can-do attitude and happy nature. She didn't know them well, like Ritchie, but they were clearly an amazing pair.

Ritchie was back in the room now, his face ashen. He put his phone back into his pocket and sat down heavily on the bed. 'It's them all right,' he said grimly. 'The authorities think they've been kidnapped along with two fellow students.' He paused, as if he was trying to take in the magnitude of what he was saying. 'Apparently the police and army have been scouring the surrounding area for two days and they haven't found a trace of either the students or the kidnappers. There's no word of them, no request for a ransom, nothing.' He rubbed his eyes and turned to Cate despairingly. 'It's unreal. Totally unreal. Somehow four people have just vanished into thin air.'

Chapter 5

The small navy-blue sports car wound its way steadily along the narrow coastal road, its soft top down to let in the cool night air, the bright headlights picking out the ocean to the left, the mountains to the right.

Sitting deep in the low leather seat, Cate could smell the salty breeze and hear the swish of the rolling ocean far below her. The wind blew gently on her face, her hair tugging and struggling to escape from its ponytail as the car accelerated around the bends.

Cate tipped her head back, gazed up at the stars huge and bright in the sky above her, and sighed. At any other time this would have been an idyllic moment – a beautiful starry night and a good-looking guy driving her up to Malibu.

But right now, Cate was struggling with a terrible sense of foreboding. It was awful to think of Amber and Jade kidnapped in a strange country, frightened, not knowing whether they would live or die.

She looked over at Ritchie. He had been mostly silent since they set off for his uncle's house but now he noticed her looking at him.

'Thanks for coming with me, Cate,' he said. 'You really didn't have to. It's just that I remember Amber and Jade saying that you were really good in a crisis and I have a feeling we're going to need all the help we can get in the next few days. Amber told me that you actually saved someone who was being attacked by a shark at the turtle sanctuary. Respect!'

Cate felt herself blushing. None of the students at the turtle sanctuary knew what had actually happened in Australia – except Michel, who had forced Cate to tell him. The others were fed a cover story. They certainly didn't know that Cate was an agent for IMIA.

'How long till we get to your uncle's house?' she said, changing the subject.

Ritchie glanced down at the small clock in the walnut dashboard. 'Fifteen minutes,' he guessed. 'We don't want to be too early. My uncle is having a few industry people over for drinks and I promised we wouldn't disturb him until they had gone. That said, here in LA, people love their beauty sleep more than they love a party. Most of the locals are tucked up in bed by ten. So if we get there for nine we should have Uncle Jack to ourselves.'

'It's really good of him to be so interested about the twins. Does he know them well?' Cate asked.

'Just through me, I guess. He helps out lots of my friends who are struggling, by paying for their books or foreign study trips. When Amber and Jade got this opportunity to go down to Mexico, Uncle Jack covered their expenses so that lack of money wouldn't stop them taking the opportunity of a lifetime.'

Cate was touched. 'That's fantastic, Ritchie,' she said. 'You must be so proud of him.'

Ritchie nodded. 'He's the best. He's looked after my mom –

his sister – and me ever since my dad died when I was a kid.' He smiled. 'He knows just about everyone there is to know in this city. He can pick up the phone and talk to the top cops, the best lawyers, even the governor of California if he has to. If anyone can find out just what is going on, he can. When we know more, we can make some sort of decision about what to do next. Amber and Jade don't have much family who can help. Their dad left them years ago and their mum has MS. She's pretty frail at the best of times and she sounded desperate on the phone when I spoke to her this evening. I gave her my word that I would do everything I could to help them, and I meant it.'

They sped on, the mountains looming high above them, tall pines casting shadows over the road. The damp smell of the forest mingled with the smell of ocean below them. It was an invigorating mix and suddenly Cate felt alert, awake and ready for action.

They turned on to a seriously smart residential road. High walls were interrupted only by entrance gates, through which Cate caught glimpses of large villas, tennis courts and huge floodlit swimming pools.

Ritchie slowed down, turned into a driveway, and stopped by a guardhouse. A CCTV camera rotated and clicked above them, and a smartly uniformed middle-aged man poked his head out of a window hatch.

'What's your name and who ya visiting?' He was polite but abrupt, only breaking into a smile when he recognised Ritchie. 'Hey, Ritchie.' He waved Ritchie on down the narrow street.

'Wow,' said Cate. 'Is it always like this?'

'You ain't seen nothing.' Ritchie grinned. 'There's an actual cop station at the west end of this street. This is Malibu Colony – wall-to-wall Hollywood royalty. Anyone who is anyone in show business has either had a house, has a house or is hoping to buy a house here. Whoopi Goldberg, Tom Hanks, Sting, Pierce Brosnan, Halle Berry . . . and people like that don't rest easy unless they have a small army watching over them.

'The beach is just behind there,' Ritchie continued, pointing through a dark garden to his right. 'If they could, the residents would even stop the public going on it, but there's a public right of way below the high-tide marks. So instead they installed that guardhouse back there to stop people coming in by the road, and made sure that the local police patrol the beach at all times to keep people away from their front windows.'

'Seems a bit . . . well, paranoid,' Cate said hesitantly. She didn't want Ritchie to think that she was being rude about his uncle. 'I'd hate to live in a place which had to be patrolled night and day.'

'I know what you mean.' Ritchie nodded thoughtfully. 'But, in fairness, there are a lot of weirdos out there. And then there are the paparazzi who can make their lives a misery – these stars may be rich, beautiful and famous, but they pretty much have to spend their whole lives looking over their shoulders.'

'How horrible,' said Cate, remembering the hordes of paparazzi that had besieged Nancy just about every time she had stepped off her yacht. 'I don't think I could stand it. And to think that so many people crave fame. Look at *The X Factor* and all those celebrity reality shows full of people saying they want to be famous. If only they knew the truth of it.'

'Be careful what you wish for, eh?' Ritchie said. 'Here we are.'

In front of them a large pair of wrought-iron gates slowly opened inward on to a terracotta-tiled driveway which cut a wide circle through an endless green lawn. A large, three-storey white building rose up in front of them. Its huge windows were edged with ornate metal balconies which ran right around the house. The top floor had been built in a wave shape, with the crest running away from them and pointing out to the ocean beyond.

'If you think this looks good, you should see the beach side of the house,' said Ritchie, clearly amused at Cate's stunned expression. 'It sits on stilts and the top balcony stretches nearly out to the ocean. There's a hot tub and a pool up there – of course.'

As the car engine died away, Cate could hear people laughing and music coming from the house. A member of staff opened the enormous front door to them.

'Ritchie, Cate, great to see you.' Johnny James, immaculately dressed in a pale suit and blue shirt, was standing in the hall chatting to a group of men in pastel suits who were clutching glasses of what looked like fizzy water. Cate recognised at least two of them as film producers who had created some of the biggest film franchises in the world. Johnny broke away from the men and came over to give his nephew a hug.

'Sorry, this is going on longer than I expected,' he said. He put out his hand to Cate. 'Thanks for coming too, Cate. We might well need some extra help, especially if it's as smart and beautiful as you.'

Cate felt herself blushing. Thank goodness she had managed a last-minute change out of her jeans and T-shirt. When Ritchie had told her where they were going she had dug out her one glamorous outfit – a pale-green maxi dress, which she was now wearing with her precious LK Bennett wedges that her dad and Monique had bought her for getting great exam results.

At least she looked as if she was actually meant to be at this party, rather than someone who was just there to do the cleaning up afterwards, she thought as she gazed around at all the gorgeous women wearing designer dresses and sipping carefully at their water.

Johnny James looked down at his watch, a discreet piece of jewellery that Cate happened to know cost well over thirty thousand pounds – Johnny advertised those very same Oyster watches in all the high-end magazines and had probably got it for free. 'This will be over in half an hour tops,' he said. 'Then I'll be with you. It's a bit last minute but I've managed to assemble a small advisory team who can at least begin to help us. There's a cop coming who specialises in kidnap, my lawyer is due any minute and we've got a call coming back from a pal who happens to be the editor of the biggest Mexican TV news station. In the meantime, make yourselves at home.' He smiled at them once more, and then he was back off into the party, shaking hands and kissing cheeks as he went.

Cate watched, entranced as a thrice-winning Oscar movie star, famed for her glacial attitude to men, melted in his presence, flirting with him like the teenager she no longer was.

Cate couldn't play at being cool any longer. 'Ritchie, this is amazing. A few days ago I was at school in London in my chemistry class trying to figure out molecular structure. Now I'm at Johnny James's Malibu beach house, partying with the stars. How did that happen?'

Ritchie smiled ruefully. 'It must be a bit weird. To me he's just my Uncle Jack, my mom's kid brother. Someone who gave me piggybacks and came to watch me play softball. But then I see how people react when they're around him and it brings it home to me just how famous he really is.'

While Ritchie grabbed a couple of Cokes from a drinks tray, Cate found herself gaping at a huge Picasso on the wall. She was desperate for a closer look but Ritchie was tugging at her arm.

'Over here,' he said, steering her through a large glass door and out on to the enormous balcony. 'There's something I want to show you.'

The moon was high and bright, a frosty white jewel glittering in a dark-blue sky, beaming down a path of silvery light across the never-ending ocean. Beneath the balcony, the waves hissed and sucked rhythmically at the flat white sand, sending tiny flumes of froth shimmering towards them.

'It's stunning,' said Cate quietly. 'Absolutely stunning.' She looked up at Ritchie. 'If I lived here, I don't think I'd need the rest of the house. I'd just camp out on this balcony and stare at the view.'

Ritchie put his arm around her and gave her a hug. 'You are one of a kind, Cate,' he said into the top of her head. 'Most girls I bring here want to hang out in the Jacuzzi or stare at the celebs. You just want to look at the view.'

'That sounds like our Cate.'

The deep voice at her shoulder made her jump. It was English, with a northern edge, almost flat-toned.

She turned slowly and, eyes widening, looked up at that familiar beak nose and huge dark eyes set in a pale face topped with floppy black hair.

'Of all the gin joints in all the towns,' he said, putting on a fake nineteen-fifties American accent, 'you walk into mine.'

'Lucas!' she said, unable to believe her eyes. Then as he smiled down at her she felt her own face breaking into the most enormous grin. 'It's so good to see you! This is beyond amazing,' she said finally.

Ritchie stared from one to the other. 'You two know each other?' he asked. 'Cate, you know Lucas Black, from Black Noir? Wow!'

'Sure does,' said Lucas, not taking his eyes off Cate's face. 'She's kind of like my lucky mascot. So I hope you don't mind me asking, Cate, but what the heck are you doing here?'

Cate frowned for a second. Before she could say anything, a loud laugh and shrieking emanated from a cloud of frothy bubbles spilling over and out of the largest hot tub that Cate had ever seen.

'Hey, waiter,' someone was calling in a broad Essex accent to one of the many young men racing around with trays of drinks and canapés. 'Bring us some more champagne, there's a good boy. I can't get out of here. It's too damn cold. I'm going to have to stay here till the sun comes up.'

Cate and Lucas grinned at each other before Lucas led them over to the hot tub.

'Look who I've just found outside, admiring the view,' he said to the back of a very blond head.

Nancy Kyle looked up from the hot tub and let out a scream, which shocked even the jazz band playing in the shadows into temporary silence.

'Cate – babe! I don't believe it!'

Ignoring her earlier pronouncement, the supermodel stood up, showing off her long, lean body which was encased in a silver snakeskin bikini. She pulled Cate into a very wet and foamy hug. 'What are you doing here? I got your text, babe, but I didn't know you knew Johnny James. You *are* a dark horse!'

'I don't,' Cate said quickly. 'Not really. But this is Ritchie, his nephew. He's a friend of a friend and invited me out here.'

She changed the subject quickly. If she had to go into details it might get tricky. 'How's the fashion show going, Nancy? I must say you're looking pretty relaxed considering there's less than two weeks to go. I would have thought that you would have been up to your eyes in phone calls and emails and whatever it is you need to do to put together something like that.'

Lucas smiled. 'Cate, do you honestly think that Nancy is

actually organising the show herself? Right now she's got about fourteen assistants running their little legs off twenty-four/seven to make sure that everything is ship-shape and perfect for the big night. Nancy just has to rock up a week on Saturday looking absolutely gorgeous and collect all the plaudits for her hard work. Isn't that right, darling?'

'Delegation, Cate,' said Nancy, nodding solemnly. 'That's the key to success.'

'And she does delegate *everything*,' Lucas said dryly. 'Including writing her books, designing her children's clothes range, and coming up with recipes for her cookbook. Not to mention the childcare, the shopping, the school run, the cooking, the gardening . . .' He grinned at Nancy affectionately, taking the sting out of his words.

'Babe!' Nancy pretended to be shocked. 'Never the shopping!' She kissed Lucas on the cheek as she grabbed Cate by the hand, leading her away to a quiet spot on the balcony.

'I didn't want to say anything in front of Ritchie, but what's happened to the gorgeous Michel? Ritchie looks pretty comfortable around you. I didn't have you down as a two-timer.'

Cate blushed furiously. 'Nancy!'

'OK, OK, just asking.' Nancy grinned.

Cate shook her head, exasperated. Perhaps this was what it was like to have a big sister teasing you. 'We've split up, if you must know.' Cate tried not to sound too sad. 'Michel dumped me. And no, Ritchie is definitely not his replacement. In fact, I only met him today.'

'Oh babe!' Nancy was clearly shocked. 'You've been dumped? What's it like?'

Cate laughed out loud then. 'Thanks, Nancy. You've really cheered me up.'

'I have?' Nancy looked bewildered. 'Well, whatever. Glad to help. What are you doing in LA, anyway?'

'I'm here to visit Mum. I haven't seen her for ages. I'm so looking forward to being with her.'

'Sweet,' said Nancy. 'Tell you what. Why don't you invite your mum out with us tomorrow night for dinner? Bring Ritchie too if you like.'

'Nancy, that would be fantastic. But if you don't mind I think I'll leave Ritchie out of it. I don't want you getting the wrong idea again. Or him for that matter. Can I check with Mum and get back to you tomorrow? She's got a new man and, knowing my mum, he might just take precedence over the daughter she hasn't seen for over a year! Where were you planning on going by the way?'

'Not sure,' said Nancy, carelessly. 'Probably won't decide until about five o'clock. Text me, babe. You know what I'm like, I might forget. Busy delegating, you see,'

CHAPTER 6

Four people were sitting around the table in Johnny's office in the basement of the house. It was windowless and, with its spartan office furniture and beige walls, it seemed a world away from the luxury just above them.

'Sorry about the dungeon,' Johnny said apologetically to Cate as he poured them all coffee. 'I can't work anywhere with a view, otherwise I spend all my time staring out of the window.'

He was seated next to Ritchie. On his other side, his lawyer, Ned – a solid-built man with piercing blue eyes under heavy lids – was shuffling quietly through bits of paper.

There was a knock and a neat-looking young man in a suit and holding a small grey folder came into the room. He nodded at the table and sat down without speaking.

'Dave Osbourne.' The lawyer waved a hand in his direction. 'The Los Angeles Police Department sent him. Apparently he's some sort of overseas crime liaison officer, brought in when an American citizen is a victim of serious crime in Mexico and Central America. His expertise is providing the link between the families and the Mexican authorities, usually in cases of kidnap or murder, and he has the thankless task of trying to persuade the Mexican police to keep the families informed and up to date with developments.'

Dave cleared his throat and nodded. 'The US Embassy in Mexico City send their apologies,' he said. 'They couldn't get anyone up here at such short notice. But they asked to be kept informed.'

There was a pause. Cate could hear the air conditioning humming and felt cold in her summer dress.

'Amber and Jade were staying at El Tajin, in the Veracruz region on the Gulf of Mexico, along with two other archaeology students,' Ritchie began. 'They were just coming to the end of working on a dig and were having a great time. Earlier this week Amber texted me to say she had found something really special, but said she couldn't talk about it yet. To be honest I didn't take that much notice – she always gets excited about every little scrap of metal or pottery she digs up and usually it turns out to be nothing.' He gave a quick smile. 'That's part of Amber's charm – her enthusiasm for everything she does.' There was a pause. 'That's all I knew really,' he continued, 'until I saw the newsflash on TV. I spoke to their mum who asked if Uncle Jack could step in and do what he could to help find them.'

'Thanks, Ritchie,' said his uncle, turning to the policeman. 'Dave?'

The man from the LAPD shuffled his papers. 'The head of the dig, a Norwegian called Stefan Vilander, had contacted the professor of archaeology from Mexico City University asking her to fly down and check something out. It was odd though: even though they had worked together for several years – the professor was even grading his PhD – Stefan refused to tell her exactly what it was they had found. He said he didn't want to risk emails and photographs being forwarded or intercepted and likewise he wouldn't talk to her further on the phone. He wanted her to see the findings first, without prejudice or warning, and go from there. She had enough respect for him to trust that he wouldn't call her down on a wild goose chase, but she was on a dig in a remote part of Ethiopia and it took her nearly a week to get back to Mexico. She was due to arrive at the site on Wednesday.' He stopped and took a sip of water. 'Apparently by the time the professor turned up, both the security guards and the students were missing,' continued Osbourne.

He glanced down at his notes again. 'The police initially carried out an extensive search of the site, widening it to a ten-kilometre radius into the rainforest around it, sending up army helicopters with thermal imaging devices, and sniffer dogs too.

He looked around the table. 'They've picked up nothing. There's been no word from them nor any sighting since. The police don't even know if the guards were part of the kidnap gang or if they were victims too. What's more, whatever it was that the students found, well, there was no sign of that, either.' He shrugged. 'Maybe the students got excited about nothing, as Ritchie suggested. Whatever the case, that's about all we know – or have been allowed to know – so far.'

Johnny turned to his lawyer. Cate wasn't sure if it was the bright light in the office or worry, but Johnny suddenly looked much older. 'What've you got, Ned?'

The big man looked grim. 'The Mexican government have now imposed a total news blackout which means that all media are being kept away from both the site and the search. They say it's to prevent the search from being impeded by the media spotlight. More likely it's because they don't want to damage their tourist industry. The site is already open again to the public.

'It's a blow for us, no doubt about it. The journalists are usually the ones with the great local contacts, but most of them will be pulled back now. If the newspapers can't cover the story, they're not going to waste the manpower investigating it. I've spoken to some colleagues who practise law over the border. Kidnapping is a growth industry in Mexico right now. Most of it is drug-related – gang on gang – or revenge, but we can probably rule that out in this case. It's my guess that this one is for money. In Mexico, even the poorest Yank is rich.' He sighed. 'I guess those kids were a prime target.'

'Has there been a ransom request?' Johnny asked eventually. 'Whatever you need, I'll do my best to raise it. Or should we offer a reward for information?'

The man from the LAPD looked horrified. 'With all due respect,' he said, 'that's the last thing we should be talking about. If the kidnappers get a whiff that their captives have rich friends, the ransom demand will go through the roof. Anyway,' he continued in his quiet drawl, 'in these cases we normally get word from the kidnappers within forty-eight hours or so. I'm going to have to disagree with you, sir.' He looked over at the lawyer. 'My belief is that the longer time goes on without contact, the less likely it is that money is the motive. Which is, I'm afraid, bad news.'

Cate listened to what he said. She couldn't help thinking Dave Osbourne looked familiar. She looked at him more closely, noting his thick dark hair, his thin lips, the nondescript grey eyes that constantly moved from person to person watching, observing, assessing. For a few seconds their eyes met but there was no hint of recognition.

'What about sending in American special forces to look for

them, Uncle Jack? Or even a private company – the ones that specialise in kidnaps?' Ritchie said.

Dave shook his head. 'Maybe, but not yet. To be honest, things are pretty touchy between the US government and the Mexicans right now. Our government has been leaning heavily on them to get their house in order over their drug trade, and in return the Mexicans are getting pretty defensive about outside interference. We can't go charging in like a bunch of cowboys to the rescue. Then there's the logistics. The region where the students went missing is covered with dense jungle, hills and a network of caves. You could send in an entire US army division, have them search for weeks, and still not find a soul.'

A discreet buzz from a phone somewhere near Johnny broke the rather despondent silence that followed.

'Excuse me.' He hit the call button and listened intensely. He spoke rapidly in Spanish – so rapidly that Cate struggled to make sense of what Johnny was saying. She heard something about theft, treasures, Americans, before he finally hung up and turned to the table.

'That was my journalist friend in Mexico City with some interesting news,' he explained. 'Before the news blackout was introduced, they had prepared a story on El Tajin. He says that there have been rumours for months of heists on other sites all over Mexico – objects stolen from museums and site exhibitions, and taken by truck to the coast where they're then smuggled out of the country by sea. The government were denying this and every time he tried to contact the sites himself, he was stonewalled. He put all his correspondents on alert, briefing them to listen out for anything that might point towards whether the rumours were true. He'd got a call from his man in Veracruz, the closest big city to El Tajin. It appears that over the few days between Stefan calling the professor and the students going missing, the locals claim a group of strangers arrived at the local town in a convoy of black pick-ups. They kept themselves to themselves, didn't eat in any of the bars, and spent their time holed up in a small hotel. The evening before the twins were reported missing, they checked out and paid their hotel bills in cash. I think we can assume the names they gave at the hotel were fake. All the hotel can tell us is that at least one of them had a US accent and another was almost certainly European.'

He paused and looked at Ritchie. 'I'm sorry to say this about your friends, but the locals are convinced that the students haven't been kidnapped. The word is that they had found treasure and were stealing it from the site and selling these artefacts to their American friends, and then something went wrong. They reckon the students and their accomplices had to make a quick getaway back over the US border. In short, the locals don't think the twins are innocent kidnap victims – they think they're partners in a terrible crime.'

'No way!' It was too much for Ritchie. 'The twins would never be mixed up in something like that. Uncle Jack, you know Amber and Jade.'

His uncle held up his hand. 'Sure, it's almost certainly just a local rumour, but the trouble with these rumours is that they sometimes have a way of catching on. Before you know it, people believe that they're the truth. I should know, I've been at the receiving end of enough of them. But even so, Ritchie, you must stay away from this. I don't want you getting involved in anything criminal.

'I'm not giving up on your friends,' he said, seeing the look on Ritchie's face. 'But let's leave it to the professionals. Ned and I will make damn sure that the police keep on looking for those kids and doing everything they can to find them.'

There was a silence and then, when it was clear no one had anything else to say, Johnny James stood up. 'I'm sorry, folks, I think we're done here. I've got a conference call coming in from my agent and my production company in a few minutes and I can't keep them waiting. I'm within a whisker of signing one of the biggest film deals ever in the history of Hollywood and I don't want to lose it.' He smiled.

Cate bit her lip and forced a smile in return. She was learning fast. This was LA, after all, where the chance to make big bucks took precedence over everything, even kidnap. She headed towards the door, which Johnny gallantly held open for her.

Standing in the hallway, Cate noticed a narrow, white door opposite. A security keypad was attached to the door frame beside it – Cate spotted the eye-recognition screen. Serious stuff.

'Uncle Jack's panic room,' said Ritchie quietly, as he joined her in the hall. 'The place he heads to, clutching his paintings and valuables, in the event of a war, hurricane, tsunami, or just plain old-fashioned larceny. Apparently it's bombproof, waterproof, fireproof and stocked with its own water, air and food supply. Not to mention a mean-looking armoury. For defence purposes, you understand.' He smiled down at Cate sardonically, noting her amazement. 'If you haven't got a panic room, you're no one, man! What were we just saying about the fun of being a celebrity?'

The security door opened and Cate got a glimpse of the whitewashed walls and dimmed lights beyond, before a tall, thin man stepped out into the hallway and stood with his back to the slowly closing door.

He was so pale he was almost albino. He met Cate's gaze with his icy blue eyes, and stared at her intently, statue still.

Her gaze slipped down his body and noted the tell-tale bulge at his hip. He was carrying a gun.

Johnny came up behind them and laughed. 'I see you've met Novak, my head of personal security. Novak, this is Cate, a friend of Ritchie's. We've been discussing the disappearance of the twins.'

The man inclined his long, narrow head towards Cate as a way of greeting, but stayed silent.

'He's not very talkative,' said Johnny, 'but he has one heck of a pedigree. Brought up in Prague, when the iron curtain fell he worked for the CIA, then MI5 and other security organisations he can't even tell me about. He's the real thing, although he does cost me a fortune – right, Novak?'

Cate thought she caught a flicker of annoyance in those icy eyes. She wasn't surprised. She would hate to be discussed, boasted about like that as if she was some prize animal picked up for the highest price.

Cate turned away from Novak and changed the subject. 'I've just had a thought. Could my father be of any use? He's Graeme Carlisle, a UN diplomat. He knows people all over the world and he's been involved in resolving kidnappings and worked alongside private security experts. At least he'll know who the best people are to contact for advice.'

'Is that right?' Johnny said slowly. 'What an interesting girl you are, Cate.' He glanced almost imperceptibly over her head towards Novak, and Cate saw, out of the corner of her eye, the security guard shake his head in a tiny movement.

'Let me talk it over with Ned.' Johnny was suddenly jovial again. 'It's a great idea but maybe we should keep this as tight as possible – for now at least. But thanks for the offer, anyway. Your dad sounds amazing. I know who to call if I get into trouble the next time I'm protesting against human rights violations in some third-world country.'

He turned to his nephew. 'Could you show Cate back upstairs, Ritchie? I'll catch up with you real soon. Cate, it's been a pleasure.'

He pressed the lift button and instantly the door slid quietly open and Cate and Ritchie stepped inside.

As they waited for the lift doors to shut, Cate glanced over at the security entrance to see Novak still staring at her, his expression unfathomable, his blue eyes now almost lifeless. Even when the lawyer crossed the hallway and whispered something quietly in his ear, he didn't take his cold eyes off her. She felt a shudder of unease. That was one man she certainly wouldn't like to cross.

As Ritchie nosed the car out of the narrow lane and on to the highway, the last of the moon disappeared behind the scudding clouds. Apart from the beams of the headlights, the darkness was cut only by the overhead road lamps, which became more and more spaced out as the car headed south out of Malibu.

Ritchie had been right about people going to bed early in LA. It wasn't even midnight and the road was pretty much empty. In Europe the streets and bars would still be heaving with people.

As they left Malibu, the road swung out towards the ocean. Cate's side of the car was just a metre or so away from the edge of the cliff, with only the crash barriers between her and the ocean far below.

Ritchie had hardly spoken since they had left the house. Cate looked over at him and tried to think of something to say that would cheer him up.

'You know what, Ritchie,' she began. 'I don't believe the twins would do anything bad either. Perhaps they got caught up in something beyond their control. Or maybe that reporter just got it completely wrong. It's just a local rumour, after all.'

Ritchie sighed. 'I told Dave Osbourne that I thought he was wrong to tell Uncle Jack to back off from offering a reward. I even threatened to go to the papers. He wasn't very pleased, I can tell you. He said I could put the twins in even more danger and I guess he has a point – not that I was going to give him the satisfaction of telling him that. Now I don't know what to do,' Ritchie continued. 'Do I leave it like Uncle Jack says or should I go down to Mexico, even if I don't know what I could really do there? But surely that's what a real friend would do.'

Cate thought for a minute. 'You know what, Ritchie? I think you should sleep on it,' she said. 'You're exhausted. In the meantime, I'm going to get my brother Arthur on the case.'

Ritchie looked at her quizzically. 'Your brother? Is he like a cop or a soldier or something?'

'No.' Cate giggled. 'He's fourteen years old, but he is just the most awesome computer whizz ever. He's got this amazing network of contacts that spreads around the world. You have no idea just how many geeks are out there, tapping away at their computers, twenty-four/seven, all them experts in one area or another, and loving any technical challenge, especially if it's something they aren't meant to be doing . . . According to Arthur, you can solve almost any problem in the world by going online. It's just a question of accessing the right person. I've learned never ever to underestimate Arthur and his mates, and boy, has he got me out of trouble a few times.'

'Well,' said Ritchie, 'why not? Let me know if he comes up with anything.'

Cate had already toyed with the idea of calling Marcus, her

IMIA handler to ask him for his help – after all, the archaeological site was close to the sea, and the rumour mentioned the illegal ocean transport of artefacts. But she had quickly dismissed the idea, at least for now. IMIA's brief was indeed to take on maritime investigation, but they only dealt with massive crimes that brought down governments, rocked stock markets and started wars. Rumours of the theft of a few artefacts and the disappearance of four students hardly fitted that bill.

Cate thought longingly of the gorgeous deep bed waiting for her back at the hotel. She yawned and glanced over at Ritchie.

He was staring at the rear-view mirror, an anxious expression on his face,

'Everything OK? asked Cate.

'Mmm, yeah I think so . . .' He was hesitant, taking his foot off the accelerator and slowing right down. 'It's just that this car has been behind us pretty much all the way since we left Malibu. When we slow down, it slows down. We speed up and it does too.' Ritchie wrinkled up his nose. 'It does seem odd that it hasn't passed us on the two-lane section.'

'Maybe the driver's just cautious,' Cate said. She fought the temptation to turn around and check the car out. 'What kind of car is it?'

'It's some kind of pick-up. Dark colour. I can't see the licence plate.'

Cate could feel her heart beginning to beat just a little faster. They hadn't passed another car for a good few minutes and she was beginning to realise just how isolated they were.

Ritchie took a sudden left off the highway, the little car rocking as it almost skidded on to a side road. The pick-up truck carried on, roaring up the highway. Cate breathed a sigh of relief, but kept watching over her shoulder and caught sight of brake lights flaring in the darkness. It had passed too quickly for her to catch the number plate, but Cate saw the large tractor-like wheels and an oversized rear bumper. It was just like the truck she had seen outside Mexicano Magic.

'Well, whoever it was has gone now,' said Ritchie, pulling back out on to the road.

Cate gave herself a mental shake. One of the downsides of her recent adventures was that she now had a tendency to read far too much into perfectly ordinary everyday events. There must be hundreds of trucks in LA that looked like that and certainly a whole stack of idiot drivers too.

They were just through the first in a series of sharp bends when there was an ear-splitting crunch and the car leaped forward through the air before crashing back down on to the road. The impact shot through Cate's body, propelling her violently forward before her seatbelt wrenched her painfully backwards into her seat.

'What the hell was that?' Ritchie was grappling with the steering wheel, trying desperately to control the car as it careered sideways across the highway.

He looked in the mirror and let out an exclamation of horror. Cate glanced in her side mirror and saw a dark, wide shape behind them – a vehicle without headlights and riding so close to them that she could hardly tell where Ritchie's car ended and this one began.

But even though the vehicle was unlit, she could still pick out the giant tractor tyres and large bull bars, which looked to her terrified mind like a giant, macabre grin.

'It's back,' she shouted above the noise of the engine revving. 'The truck that was behind us earlier. Whatever you do, don't stop!'

'Hold tight!' Ritchie yelled, and the car jerked forwards again, this time landing almost against the cliff-top barriers. Cate was ready for the impact, but even so it still sent agonising shockwaves through her body and it was all she could do not to scream out.

'Can you outrun him?' she asked.

Miraculously, the car was still moving, but it felt as if at least one of the tyres was damaged and there was an ominous grinding coming from somewhere beneath her feet.

'I'll try,' Ritchie shouted back over the noise of the engine. He stamped on the pedal and the little car gallantly pushed forwards. But a quick glance behind showed Cate that the truck was on them again, this time pushing rather than crashing into them, forcing the car nearer and nearer to the cliff edge and the long sheer drop to the ocean below.

They're trying to push us over the cliff, thought Cate, cold fear twisting in her stomach. They're trying to kill us! But why? Her mind was racing, trying to make sense of the madness. Was it her they were after? Or Ritchie? Or was it a case of mistaken identity?

Cate was just reaching into her bag for her phone when she saw a road sign up ahead, reminding drivers that they were coming up to a picnic area.

'Turn in,' she yelled, pointing to the sign. 'Turn in there, Ritchie, we can't outrun them – it's our only hope of losing them.'

He stared at her blankly, his eyes faint and distant.

'Ritchie,' she said again, more urgently, 'listen to me. Concentrate. Come on, Ritchie, please.'

Then she saw the blood. Lots of it, coursing down the left side of his head, falling on to his pale shirt.

Her heart sank and she gave another despairing glance behind her. The truck had dropped back slightly. Getting ready for another attack, she thought grimly, then looked up ahead. There were no other cars around, no last-minute saviour on the horizon. She was on her own.

The gap in the barrier was nearly on them and Cate made up her mind. Taking a deep breath she moved over towards Ritchie as far as her seatbelt would let her, grabbed the wheel with her left hand and with her right pulled hard on the handbrake.

'Brake, Ritchie brake!' she screamed in his ear as she yanked hard at the wheel and somehow Ritchie heard her and understood, pushing his right leg forward on the brake, hurtling the car into a skid.

There was an angry scrape of metal on tarmac and Cate's nostrils were filled with the hot, dirty stench of burning rubber. She released the handbrake, her other arm screaming from the effort of holding the wheel in lock, but somehow, amazingly, the car made it through the gap in the barrier, careered down a slope and along a wide gravel path before finally coming to a halt in the grassy parking area.

'Ritchie, get out – get out of the car!' Cate was already looking over her shoulder. Unable to stop, the truck had gone roaring on up the road, but she knew it was only a matter of moments before it U-turned back on the empty highway.

Ritchie's head lolled as he tried to look at her. 'Sorry,' he said. He was fighting to keep his eyes open. 'Sorry. Feel bad. Really bad. Leave me. Go.'

'No way,' said Cate, slinging her bag across her shoulders. She pushed desperately at her dented door, then, when it refused to open, swung round and kicked hard with both feet and the cool night air rushed in, cutting like a sword through the fetid smell of sweat and fear.

She jumped out and ran around the front of the car. The bumper was hanging off, half under the car, the front tyres were so shredded that there was hardly any rubber left, and smoke was seeping out from under the bonnet. The unmistakable smell of petrol hung in the air like an invisible haze.

Cate yanked at the driver's door and Ritchie almost fell on to her, his eyes closed, his body floppy. She staggered slightly under his weight, recovered her balance and slid her hand across him to undo his seatbelt, grimacing as she felt the hot, sticky liquid dripping from his forehead on to her bare arm.

She had to get him out of there. Even if the guys from the pick-up truck didn't come to finish them off, there was a very real risk of the car going up in flames.

'Ritchie!' She found herself whispering even though she knew that they were alone. 'Ritchie, please get out of here. We need to hide.'

Ritchie grunted and opened his eyes slightly. He seemed to understand. He gripped hard on her shoulder and with the other hand pushed against the steering wheel, and somehow he was out of the car and swaying slightly on his feet.

Cate could hear the growing sound of a powerful engine in the distance. Her stomach lurched.

The moon was out again now, its light revealing the dark shapes of trees and bushes set away from the parking place. If they got to some sort of cover at least they would have a chance of hiding.

Her heart pounding, Cate steered Ritchie towards the edge of the clearing, praying that he would make it without collapsing. His breathing was heavy, his legs kept buckling beneath him and every step seemed to take for ever.

Finally they were into the woods. Cate guided Ritchie into a patch of low-lying dense bushes, where he collapsed on to the ground.

She looked around. She needed something to protect them both. The noise of the approaching vehicle was loud, almost over her head. She sprinted back towards the car where an ominous glow from the underside was sending spiny flickers of smoke and flames up around the doors.

Cate yanked on the partially attached bumper. The hot metal burned her fingers but she kept going until part of it finally tore away, and she saw to her satisfaction that the broken end was jagged and sharp. She looked again at the car and an idea came to mind. She quickly slammed the doors shut before running back and diving into the bushes, just as the dark pick-up truck rolled silently down the slope towards them.

CHAPTER 7

The truck came to a halt close to Cate's hiding place and stood still, silhouetted against the moonlight, the engine sighing as it cooled down.

Hardly daring to breathe, Cate slipped her hand into her bag and switched her phone to silent. Just a few metres in front of the truck the fire had taken hold in the car, the flames licking steadily up through the floor and devouring the seats in which she and Ritchie had been sitting just a few minutes earlier.

It was eerily quiet. Only the muffled sound of crackling flames broke the silence of the night. Cate could feel her heart pounding as she waited for the occupants of the truck to make their move.

She wondered how many there were and how big and how well armed they would be. She felt the adrenalin coursing through her body, priming her for action, sharpening her wits and her senses.

Cate ran through some of her favourite mantras in her head, that she had learned in her self-defence and martial arts classes.

Attack is the best form of defence.

Surprise is everything.

Your body is a lethal weapon.
Brain beats brawn every time.

Now more than ever she needed the confidence that they had always inspired in her.

The truck door nearest to Cate opened slowly and a long pair of legs, clad in jeans and Doc Martens swung out and down on to the gravel. The man stood with his back to Cate, but his tall, thin build was clear. He walked towards the car and stood a few metres away, peering into the flame-filled interior, shuffling back as the heat became too intense.

Keeping a respectful distance, he walked around the front of the car and Cate caught a glimpse of his masked face and gloved hands. This was no prankster, this was a serious criminal who would cover his tracks. He bent down to look through the passenger-side window, but he was forced to move even further away as the flames erupted.

A voice came from the pick-up truck. 'Can you see anything? Can you see them?' It was a man talking, youngish. His accent was American but with a strong Spanish lilt.

'I can't tell.' The tall man sounded Eastern European – Polish, Czech maybe? 'It's too damn hot to get anywhere near. But the doors are shut fast, so chances are they couldn't get out when the fire started. Which means —' he laughed then, a terrible, thin sound that sent shivers down Cate's spine, '— they're probably in there right now, roasting like two spit chickens. Job done.'

Cate felt sick. It was hard to believe that anyone could be so callous.

'Well, let's trash the evidence,' the driver sounded impatient. 'By the time the cops find that car they'll have no idea what happened to it, let alone the kids inside.'

The tall man stood back from the truck as the engine revved

73

and growled, like a bull waiting to charge. The truck rolled forward until it was bumper to bumper with the blazing car, then Cate watched with a mixture of sadness and horror as it rammed the car closer and closer to the edge of the cliff.

Suddenly, from behind her, Cate heard the unmistakable sound of a mobile phone ringing. She froze. Ritchie!

It cut off almost instantly, but the tall man had heard it too. He turned on his heel and raced towards the truck, waving his arms. 'Hold it,' he shouted. 'Wait.'

If he heard him, the truck driver was enjoying himself far too much to stop. There was an ear-splitting, grinding noise from the edge of the cliff as the car was pushed against the crash barrier.

The man stood, his head cocked, listening for another ring. Cate crossed her fingers, praying that the answerphone system hadn't been triggered.

She held her breath, feeling the sweat trickling down the small of her back. Then, to her horror, a loud bleep signalled the text alert for a message. The man gave a last glance to the truck and then set off at a brisk trot towards where Ritchie was lying. As he headed into the darkness, Cate tightened her fingers around her makeshift weapon. She had no choice – it was time to go into battle.

Cate backed out of her cover and edged around the clearing towards where she had left Ritchie. He was lying half propped up on his elbow, his eyes open. He saw her and tried to sit up, looking at her with a dazed expression as she held her finger to her lips.

The man was heading straight for them, his masked head up like a hunting dog, his body language aggressive and angry. He lifted up his right hand. Her heart sank as she saw he was holding a small gun, carrying it ahead of him like a pro. Now all she had left on her side was the element of surprise. She had better make the most of it.

He was just a metre away from her when she struck, racing out of the darkness with her weapon raised above her. She brought the metal down hard on his shoulder, felt it make contact with his neck, and he staggered sideways then fell to his knees. The blow should have stunned him, but this man was strong and somehow he struggled to his feet. No sound came from him, but through the slits in his mask, Cate could see his eyes staring at her with an intense hatred. He brought his right hand up, the metal of the gun flashing in the darkness. Cate kicked out high with her left leg, catching his elbow and pushing his arm far above his head. The impact sent the gun flying from his hand in a backwards arc into the darkness.

The man swore angrily but Cate sensed he was weakening, not so sure about what to do next. While he wavered, she brought the metal shaft round at waist level, cracking it into his pelvis. He doubled forward and fell on to his knees, moaning. Cate brought the bumper down on his neck once more and he collapsed on to his side.

Beside her, Ritchie was staggering to his feet, a shocked expression on his face.

'Am I dreaming?' he said, staring at Cate in amazement. 'Did I just see you take on a man twice your size and bring him down?'

Cate gave him a quick grin. 'I don't make a habit of it, honestly.' She glanced at the man who was lying, face down and silent, but still clearly breathing. 'Ritchie, we have to get on to the main road fast. Our only hope is to flag down a car and get out of here. Can you walk?'

He nodded. 'After what I've just seen I think I'd better put myself completely in your hands.'

The truck had reversed back up the clearing. The driver was obviously waiting for his partner to return. 'Hey, big man,' he shouted. The voice sounded irritated, fractious, his accent more pronounced. 'Come on, now, we need to get outta here.'

There was silence.

'Quit messing. Get your butt in here and let's go.' He got out of the truck, leaving the engine running and turned towards Cate and Ritchie, who were standing in the shadows of some pine trees.

Cate could just make out the close-shaven head, the narrow lips; and, as he came closer, she stared in horrified fascination at two metal points glinting in his chin, sticking through the flesh like nails. Despite herself, she shuddered. If this man was even a tenth as mean as he looked they could expect no mercy.

He kept walking towards them. For one dreadful moment Cate thought he had spotted them, but he veered around the truck and headed back towards the edge of the clearing.

An idea was forming in Cate's mind. 'Are you up to driving?' she whispered in Ritchie's ear. He stared down at her in surprise and then, as he understood what she was saying, he nodded. 'Yep. Pick-ups are my speciality.'

Cate raced to the truck and Ritchie stumbled after her. He headed for the driver's side as Cate threw herself into the passenger seat. Within seconds, Ritchie reversed up out of the clearing. Then he slammed on the brakes, rammed the gearstick into first, and slapped his foot hard to the ground. As the truck hurtled forward, Cate saw the man stop, turn on his heel and start to run back towards them.

Cate wound down the window and, iPhone in hand, aimed the lens carefully at their pursuer, pressed the button and a flash lit up the sky.

He drew closer as the truck picked up speed. 'Drop the phone, kid,' the man screamed after her, 'or you're dead! Drop it!'

'I don't think so, mate!' said Cate, resisting the urge to wave as

76

Ritchie roared up the road. Cate sat back in her seat and examined the picture of the man, noting with satisfaction how the two metal points had caught the flash. 'Not a bad shot, considering the circumstances,' she said to Ritchie proudly.

It was past midnight by the time they reached the Santa Monica police station, but the main waiting room was packed. There was a gang of disgruntled kids, a surprisingly tuneful drunk warbling his way through 'We'll Meet Again', and a middle-aged couple who were arguing furiously about whose turn it was to bail out their daughter yet again.

Ritchie and Cate picked their way through the mayhem towards the reception. To Cate's utter dismay, it was still the same sergeant on duty. When she saw Cate, her expression turned from one of bored indifference to surprise and then pure malice.

'You in trouble again, kid?' she said, ignoring Ritchie.

'I didn't know you were a regular here, Cate.' Ritchie shot Cate a half-amused, half-questioning glance. The blood on his face had dried and, although he was still pale, his eyes were now brighter and alert.

'Look, ma'am,' he said, turning to the sergeant, 'my name is Ritchie Daner and I'm a second-year med student at UCLA. We're here to report a crime. My friend and I here were pursued and rammed on the Santa Monica highway and someone tried to kill us. We managed to escape in their pick-up. It's parked right outside. Here's the licence plate details.' He shoved a piece of paper across the desk. 'Surely you can find out who owns it and catch them from that. In any case, they're probably still where we left them, at the highway pull-in close to Topanga Beach.'

The sergeant turned to stare at Ritchie, taking in his dishevelled appearance and battered face. 'OK, son,' she said finally. 'Start again, slowly. The truth, the whole truth, and nothing but the truth, or you'll wish you never set foot in this building.'

'Tell them what happened, Cate.' Ritchie turned to her.

But Cate wasn't looking at him any longer. Her gaze had shifted to the other side of the waiting room, where Dave Osbourne had just walked in through the large glass doors.

'Cate, Ritchie, what's going on here? You OK?'

Next to Ritchie, Dave's slender frame looked even less substantial yet there was, Cate thought, a toughness about him, an inner hardness that she recognised.

'Sir, these kids say they're the victims of dangerous pursuit and intent to harm,' said the sergeant, suddenly respectful. 'I was just checking out their story.' She paused, her eyes wary behind her glasses. 'You know them, sir?' she asked.

Dave nodded brusquely. 'Sure do,' he said.

'They want me to send some cops out to the Topanga Beach pull-in and look for two males. They've got the licence plate of the truck the men were driving. It's parked outside.'

'Well, what are you waiting for?' Dave asked her. 'Get some men out there and get forensics on to the truck. Run the licence through the usual channels – and Sergeant,' he continued, 'call the doctor, now. I want someone to look at this boy's head. In the meantime, I'll talk to this young lady and find out what's been going on.'

The sergeant glanced nervously at a chart on the wall beside her. 'You can use the small meeting room.' She picked up a phone. 'I'll call the doctor in right away.'

'Make sure we're not disturbed,' said Dave, taking Cate by the elbow and steering her through the crowds towards the room. He turned to Ritchie, who was still following them. 'Head injuries can be dangerous things, you need to get it checked out,' he said to the younger man firmly, gesturing towards the sergeant. 'Wait there. The doc is on his way. Once he's given you the all-clear, come and find us.'

The room was hardly bigger than a cupboard, airless, windowless, and only a single overhead bulb lit the two, dirty, brown chairs. It smelled of dust and chewing gum.

Dave leaned against the wall and gestured for Cate to sit down. As she did, Cate suddenly realised she was totally shattered, the adrenalin that had kept her alert over the last hour finally deserting her.

She stared blearily up at Dave, forcing herself to concentrate. His dark slicked-back hair gleamed in the harsh light, his grey-eyed gaze never wavered from her face.

And then she remembered. It was in Australia a few months ago. She was in her diving gear, onboard a small rubber dinghy, headed out towards the island where the Cotian criminals were hiding their kidnap victim and plotting their assault on Snapper Bay. The diver next to her gave her last-minute instructions on her equipment in the same soft Californian drawl – and had later dragged her exhausted body back out of the dark water and wrapped her in a blanket whilst Henri lectured her on her recklessness. There could be no mistake: Dave was no LAPD cop. He was an IMIA agent.

'How's Marcus?' she asked him suddenly. 'And Henri?' I haven't heard from them in a while.'

Dave looked at her thoughtfully. 'I wondered how long it would take before you recognised me,' he said quietly. 'Marcus said a few hours, Henri reckoned a day. They send their regards by the way.'

'Thanks!' said Cate sarcastically. As usual the IMIA always seemed to be one step ahead of her. 'And what about you? What was your estimation of my brilliance – or lack of it?'

'Me?' Dave smiled then. 'I honestly thought you had me rumbled after ten minutes in Johnny James's office. After all, your reputation does go before you.'

She shook her head. 'I don't believe it!' she exclaimed. Her tiredness was gone now, replaced by a growing indignation. 'I come to LA for a holiday, a proper holiday for the first time in ages, and before I know it I'm locked in a bunker and then some maniacs in a pick-up truck try to kill me. To cap it all, I end up bumping into an IMIA agent. Talk about a string of bad luck. No offence,' she added hastily.

'None taken,' said Dave gravely. 'I can quite understand that after the last investigation you might want a break from IMIA. You did a fantastic job. Well, you and Arthur both did, and as much as we would love to have you working for us full time, we appreciate you may not feel quite the same way.' He paused and then sighed. 'However, Cate, things aren't quite what they seem. What you may think are amazing coincidences, well – let's just say we've been keeping an eye on you ever since you arrived in LA. For a very good reason.'

His phone rang. 'Hold on,' he said as he took the call.

Cate's mind was a fuzz of random thoughts. As Dave muttered into his phone, she tried hard to concentrate. Why would IMIA be keeping an eye on her? She was on holiday for goodness' sake. And what was Dave doing undercover in LA – and at Johnny James's house?

The call over, Dave stared at Cate, a serious expression on his face. 'They've traced the owner of the truck. Am I right in thinking that the name "Burt Tyler" means something to you?'

CHAPTER 8

Cate lay stretched out on the large bed, watching the early-morning surfers playing like dolphins out in the ocean, marvelling as they swooshed and swooped over the silvery-blue swell before gliding in to the white sand.

For a few minutes she allowed herself to be drawn into their acrobatics, fantasising about taking a walk to the surf school and signing up for lessons.

She grinned wryly to herself. Fat chance of that now. After the events of the previous day, a laid-back fun-filled holiday seemed even further away than ever.

Dave Osbourne had dropped Cate off at the hotel with an ominous, 'We'll see you tomorrow,' and while she had been way too tired to even query his remark she knew exactly what that meant. He – and IMIA – weren't finished with her yet.

She checked her phone. There were several texts from Arthur telling her to call him and one from Ritchie which very sweetly asked if she was OK, making no mention of his own head injury. Cate smiled. She was beginning to really like that guy. She had a message too, a number she didn't recognise. She dialled voicemail and then sat up in shock as Johnny James's silkily smooth tones purred into her ear.

'Cate, Ritchie told me about your awful experience last night. I am so, so sorry that this happened to you after you left my house. Thank God you are safe. Novak has had to make an emergency family visit to New York, but as soon as he gets back I assure you he will be on the case and I promise we'll leave no stone unturned in looking for the culprits. In the meantime, please, please, if you need anything – anything at all – don't hesitate to call me on this number.'

Wow, thought Cate, a girl really couldn't ask for a better start to the day. Johnny James being concerned about her! Unable to help herself, Cate listened to the message four times before catching sight of her stupidly grinning face in the mirror and pulling herself together. She pushed back the soft linen sheets and headed for the bathroom where, for a good ten minutes, she soaked herself under the power shower, listening to the local radio, smiling at the cheery, upbeat style of the presenter.

Back in the room, she pulled on her soft tracksuit bottoms and a T-shirt, and rummaged around for her tablet in her rucksack. She juiced up a mango, a banana and a punnet of blueberries she found in the fridge, pouring in a tub of natural yogurt to complete her breakfast concoction.

Perfect, she thought, taking an appreciative slurp as she carried the tall glass out on to the already-warm balcony.

She sat down in one of the deep wicker baskets facing the sun, flicked on her tablet, and headed for Amber's Facebook page. It was time to do some research.

For twenty minutes or so, Cate scoured Amber's page. She had around two hundred and fifty friends, but as far as Cate could see they were mainly fellow students and some eco-warriors. Cate also had a friend request from Ritchie on her page, which she accepted. She noted, with a strange feeling of satisfaction, his status was single.

Next, Cate looked at Amber's wall. It seemed to be made up of the usual gossip, personal messages to friends, the odd snippet of news about the dig and how hard, yet satisfying, it was. Cate kept looking for something – anything – that would give some clue about what had led to the students' disappearance. Then she noticed that on Monday there was a posting saying, *The best day EVER, yesterday. I'll remember it for the rest of my life.* Ritchie had said she'd been very excited when she texted him. What had happened on Sunday?

She logged on to Twitter. The last tweet by Jade had been on Tuesday at nine p.m. local time, just a few hours before she disappeared, Cate reckoned. It was nothing special, just a happy birthday message for a fellow tweeter and before that a mention of a fab fish meal she had cooked. Cate scrolled back down through the tweets. Jade had been reasonably prolific, sometimes tweeting up to six or seven times a day – mostly on mundane matters: the weather, the wildlife she had seen, the things she was missing about home. Nothing stood out and Cate was just about to give up when suddenly one tweet, posted on Sunday, caught her eye.

Thor was so wrong, yet so right. All will be revealed shortly twerps.

Cate stared at the message, trying to make sense of it. And who – or what – was Thor? He was the Viking god of war, Cate knew, and it was a common Scandinavian name. But how did that relate to anything? Or was it even mistyping?

Cate blew out her cheeks and switched off the tablet. It was time for a break. She drank the last few drops of her smoothie and sat back in the chair, feeling the sun on her face. She breathed deeply, enjoying the sensation of the fresh ocean air in her lungs and felt herself relaxing, drifting slowly back to sleep.

She woke with a start. A screeching, bellowing noise roared through the powerful speakers and out on to the balcony.

For a few crazy seconds she was convinced she was hallucinating. Then she jumped to her feet and, hands over her ears, stumbled back into her room. Perched on the white leather stool behind the mixing desk, his dark face framed with the Beat headphones, glowing with pride and sporting a grin from ear to ear was none other than Marcus, her handler, the man who had introduced her to IMIA.

Cate paused, marched over to the mixing desk and, without a word, leaned behind it and pulled out the plug. As the silence fell on the room, Marcus's face took on a hurt expression.

'Hey, Cate,' he said mournfully. 'You trashed my sounds. Just as I was getting into the swing of it as well.'

Cate shot him a withering look. 'I'd like to know just what you think you're doing breaking into my room? It's illegal, in case you didn't know. And how on earth did you know I was here, anyway? Ohhh, I get it. Did Dave Osbourne call you?'

Marcus pulled off his headphones reluctantly. 'Cate! So many questions. And not even a "Hello and nice to see you, Marcus" first.'

He got up slowly from the desk, walked over to the balcony doors and shut them.

'Marcus, I'm on holiday – visiting my mum, who will be here to pick me up any minute now.'

'No, she won't,' Marcus said calmly. 'Right now she's sitting waiting for a rescue truck on the road just north of San Diego.

Her van has had a puncture. Or rather two. Just to be on the safe side.' He chuckled. 'We wanted to make sure we had enough time to talk to you. If you check your phone you'll probably find a text from her telling you that she's been delayed for a couple of hours. Oh and how are you enjoying the Erin? It's where all the cool kids hang out, by the way – that's why we chose it for you.'

Cate sat down on the bed and frowned, remembering the Asian woman in the restaurant. Of course. That was IMIA all over, always one step ahead of her, making her feel like a complete pawn in their games.

She fought back a sharp retort. She knew that it was a waste of energy to try to fight them – it was far better to go along with them, listen to what they had to say and then find other ways of asserting herself.

There was a quiet knock at the door and Dave Osbourne came into the room. He nodded at Cate and perched himself on one of the high stools by the kitchen bar. Behind him, his familiar, solid bulk filling up the doorway, was Henri Sorenzi, former CIA, Mossad and MI5 agent and now the much revered and rather scary head of IMIA.

Whatever this is about, it must be important, thought Cate, as she watched him check out the room, his dark, piercing eyes swooping and searching around. Henri didn't usually make personal calls – people mostly came to him.

'Good morning, Cate,' Henri said finally in his perfect English accent and then, without waiting for a reply, added, 'Is the room clean, Marcus? We need to be completely sure before we talk.'

Marcus nodded. 'No bugs. Checked everywhere. Cate, here, slept through it all like a baby.'

Henri shook his head, tutting loudly. 'Bit careless, Cate. Letting Marcus walk in like that. Making sure your accommodation is secured is pretty much basic stuff for any of my agents. Must try harder.'

Cate stared at him crossly. 'Er, Henri, in case you hadn't noticed, I'm actually on holiday. And since when was I one of your agents again?'

There was a silence. Henri and Cate eyeballed each other. Cate could hear Dave Osbourne shuffling uncomfortably behind her and then, as he had done so many times before, Marcus stepped in to break the impasse.

'Hey, guys.' He juggled some oranges in the air. 'Fancy a juice while we catch up? In case you've forgotten, I'm a pretty good chef.'

Henri grunted and dropped his gaze.

'Cate, I thought you might want to know,' Dave said, 'we didn't find the thugs at Topanga beach, but the picture you took on your phone looks very similar to a mugshot we have of one Gabriel Montanez. His piercings alone gave him away. He's a nasty piece of work, well known to the cops here. Local, a hired thug, been in and out of prison since he was a kid. He's currently on probation for car theft with extreme violence. I'm told he's also a hired gun. That is, he'll do pretty much anything for money. He's not stupid, either.'

'Have you arrested him?' asked Cate.

Dave shook his head. 'He was brought in early this morning for questioning. Unfortunately he has an alibi. Well, his girlfriend said he was at home with her all evening.'

'What about the other guy? The one wearing the mask. Any news on him?'

'Nothing. Sorry. To be fair we had very little to go on and

Gabriel wasn't helping.' Dave looked annoyed. 'He knows how to play the game. Forensics are going over the pick-up, but haven't found any fingerprints. They're looking for DNA traces, but until then we only have your word and your picture of him as evidence. I'm afraid his lawyer made light work of those. Said the picture didn't give a clear location and could be fake, and that you would have been too traumatised by the road rage to be a reliable witness.'

Cate felt her hackles rising. 'So you let him go? He tried to run Ritchie and me into the ocean and you let him go?'

Dave grimaced. 'Not exactly. He's out on a pretty large bail and we've taken his passport. Don't worry, we'll get him. It may just take a little time that's all.'

As he spoke, there was an almost imperceptible tap on the door. Marcus opened it to the receptionist, her blond dreadlocks glowing in the sun that was flooding in behind her.

Cate got up. 'Sorry about the noise,' she said hurriedly. 'And, erm, these guys are friends of mine. They were just in town and popped in to say hello. They'll be going very soon.'

Behind her Henri let out a snort of amusement. 'Come in, Rosie. I would introduce you to Cate Carlisle, our youngest IMIA agent, but I believe you two have already met.'

Cate stared in amazement as the receptionist stepped into the room, closing the door behind her. Cate was still staring as she shook hands with Marcus and Dave, then sat down on the bed.

'Sorry, honey,' she said to Cate. 'I simply couldn't let you know who I was until I got the word from Marcus. I have to say it was a bit of a thrill to learn that I would be helping out on a case with Cate Carlisle! I'm Rosie Collins, by the way.'

Cate turned to Marcus who was pulling down the blinds on

the window. 'For goodness' sake,' she pleaded, 'will someone please put me out of my misery and tell me what's going on?'

The laptop flickered in the darkened room. On the screen Cate could see pictures of an ancient Mexican site, very similar to the one she and Ritchie had seen on the news the night before. The camera panned around the soaring pyramids and crept into darkened tunnels, before stopping in a large stone chamber.

In the centre of the room, a gold-covered tomb was raised up on square boulders and, as the camera zoomed in, Cate let out a gasp of amazement. Piled almost haphazardly around the base of the tomb was treasure. Terrifying death masks with eye slits inlaid with turquoise lay on top of gleaming silver drinking cups; gold-tipped spears and dull metal shields were slung side by side on a heap of gold chains and coins.

Behind the tomb, two squat young Mexican men with machine guns slung over their broad shoulders were grinning broadly at the camera, gesturing with a thumbs-up their delight at the sight in front of them.

'Wow,' said Cate to no one in particular. 'Cool. Good old-fashioned treasure.'

She heard Henri cough behind her. 'Antiquities, Cate. Found at Christmas, in a secret tomb after the excavation of a pyramid in north-west Mexico. Objects dating back well over a thousand years, some of them older than that. All made by tribes and cultures that are long gone. They are priceless things of total beauty that, by rights, belong to the Mexican people and indeed, to all of us. The find was kept top secret, with just a handful of people who lived and worked on the site knowing about it. The treasures were due to be moved to a museum to be listed and catalogued and electronically tagged before being kept in a perfect protective environment – to preserve them for us and for future generations. Then this happened.'

He stopped and reached down to the keyboard and another shot of the chamber appeared on the screen, but now the tomb was overturned, the treasure all but gone, just a few coins scattered across the floor. As the camera moved around the chamber, Cate saw with horror that the stone walls were now splattered with blood. In the corner were two bodies, their legs splayed at unnatural angles, dark stains seeping from beneath them. She looked away.

'As you can see, despite the best efforts of those two brave guards and a top-notch security system, somehow this happened.'

Cate forced herself to look at the screen again, noting the bullet holes that riddled the ceiling, the smashed stonework of the tomb. It was like a battle zone, in a darkened underground chamber. There would have been no hope of escape from the deadly bullets as they ricocheted off the walls, ripping indiscriminately through the bodies of the trapped men. She pushed the horrible image away and turned back to Henri, forcing herself to concentrate on what he was saying.

'That heist happened three months ago,' he explained gesturing at the screen, 'but between then and now there have been three other similar raids across Mexico, stealing from on-site museums or displays. The antiques have simply vanished into thin air. In the last one before El Tajin, two Mexican tourists who were camping near the site heard a noise and went to investigate. They were found dead.'

Henri sounded matter-of-fact, but Cate knew better. She had worked with IMIA long enough to know that, to them, every unnecessary death was a tragedy, every life was worth saving. That was what made them so good at their job and so sought after by every government in the world to solve their most difficult crimes.

'So then you were called in. But why IMIA? You normally only deal with maritime crimes.'

'We were already in this part of the world,' said Marcus. 'We'd heard that there was an Al Qaeda plot to blow up the entrance to the Panama Canal, but the information turned out to be dud. We were about to pack up and leave for Europe when a contact from the Mexican government approached us.'

Marcus hit the keyboard again. A map of Mexico flashed up, studded with red dots. 'Every raid has taken place on sites near to the coast,' he said, pointing at the dots. 'They wanted to explore the possibility that the antiquities may have been smuggled out by sea. We started to make enquiries, to put out feelers. Then El Tajin happened. The Mexican government is in utter panic. Up until then they managed to keep the heists quiet, but now the victims are US and European citizens. This takes it to a whole new level. It's bad enough if a tourist wanders into the wrong area of town and gets caught in some crossfire, but when the actual tourist sites become the targets – well, that's a very worrying trend. The Mexican government has seen what happened in Kenya when the Somalian bandits moved into the tourist areas. It decimated their tourist industry overnight.'

'So you don't believe that the twins – or any of the students – were involved in the crime?' Cate asked. She turned to Dave Osbourne. 'That's what Johnny James had heard.'

He shook his head slowly. 'That sounds like a rumour put about to deflect from the real truth: that this gang is becoming more and more ruthless.'

'When the students couldn't be found, we thought there was a good chance that they had been smuggled out by sea, too,' explained Marcus. 'We sent up planes, checked all suspicious shipping, even sent down specially-equipped submarines to search underwater in case they had been taken out that way. We found nothing.'

'What do you think has happened to them?' Cate asked.

Suddenly no one would look Cate in the eye.

Outside, she could hear a dog barking and children laughing as they played on the beach below them. Her room was freezing cold now, the air conditioning set far too high, the warmth of the sunshine blocked out by the blinds.

Cate looked at her watch – it was eight-twenty a.m. Less than twenty-four hours since she had landed in LA, and so much had happened. She felt as if she was at the start of a rollercoaster that was slowly but surely gathering speed, and she was stuck on it for the duration of the ride, no matter how wild and how scary it turned out to be.

'Why are you undercover at this hotel?' Cate suddenly asked Rosie, who was sitting quietly on the bed. 'What's so special about the Erin?'

Marcus, not Rosie, replied. 'When we said that the antiquities vanished into thin air, that wasn't quite right. The major pieces, sure. They haven't been seen since they were stolen. But a few weeks after the first robbery some smaller pieces – bits of jade, the odd bead necklace, a dagger – were already appearing on the black market. We put some of our internet experts on it and, sure enough, every few weeks something would pop up for sale on the dodgy trading sites where few questions are asked. At first we thought that they must be fakes. We couldn't believe that anyone would be so dumb as to start selling off the goods from these huge heists. So last week we made an offer for a brooch, agreed a cash payment of ten thousand dollars, and were sent instructions for

91

collecting it. We were told to wait outside the Erin at sundown,' he continued. 'A man arrived in his pick-up truck, came into the bar and went, as arranged, to the corner seats by the window. A good-looking guy, big, broad and very careful. He didn't show us the brooch right away – but once he thought we were for real, he handed it over. It was genuine, all right – a one-thousand-year-old Mayan brooch from one of the sites that had been attacked. He told us there was more where this came from and that if we wanted to see him again all we had to do was leave a message at the Erin's front desk. He was our one real lead, so there was no way we were going to arrest him – well, not then, anyway. So we just let him walk right out of the door and get back into his truck.'

Marcus rubbed at his eyes. He looked tired, thought Cate. Stressed. Not the usual laid-back Marcus who had held her hand and guided her through two missions, who had always been there to lift her spirits with a joke or a smile.

'I'm guessing you had him photographed and ID'd in about twenty seconds,' said Cate.

Marcus nodded. She could see the embarrassment mixed with concern on his face and, worst of all, she could see pity. She was beginning to feel sick.

'Who was he, Marcus?' she said, already dreading the answer. He opened his mouth to speak, then hesitated again.

'Don't worry,' she said. 'I'll say it for you. The man was Burt Tyler, wasn't he? My mum's boyfriend.'

Marcus nodded. 'We ID'd him as a regular at the Erin – which is why we put Rosie in place. Then we put a tail on him right away of course.' He tried to smile. 'We were just in the process of ID'ing his girlfriend when we intercepted a call from her telling Burt that her daughter, Cate Carlisle, was coming over to visit.

That was a nice surprise, a bonus we couldn't overlook.' He shot Cate an apologetic look.

'So you got my mother delayed in Mexico and led me straight to the Erin,' Cate said flatly. She was trying hard to contain her rising anger.

'You got it,' Henri said curtly. 'You know as well as we do, Cate, that, like it or not, we have to use everything at our disposal. Including a sixteen-year-old girl with an uncanny gift for spying.'

Cate started to argue, but he raised his hand.

'Yesterday you went to Mexicano Magic – Tyler's shop. Dave said you saw three men acting suspiciously and you rattled them enough for them to lock you away – even threaten to kill you. Cate, you can't hide away from this. Burt is definitely caught up in something very murky indeed.'

Cate's anger suddenly gave way to panic. 'My mother,' she said, 'do you think she's involved in any of this? Do you think she has any idea what's happening?'

'The truth is we just don't know yet.' Henri shrugged. 'So far, Burt Tyler is the only lead we've got.'

'And you're going to be closer to him than any of us could ever hope to get,' added Marcus. 'Cate, I know what we're asking of you and I understand why you would be angry that we are dragging you back into our world. But you're the best chance – maybe the only chance – we've got of stopping these dreadful crimes and of finding your friends Amber and Jade before it's too late.'

CHAPTER 9

Cate sat down on a stool next to Marcus, her mind in utter turmoil.

IMIA had asked so much of her already – she had risked her life for them, spied on her own friends, even lost her boyfriend Michel because of them. To be asked to spy on her own mother's boyfriend – and possibly even her mother – was too much. But if she didn't . . . well, the message had been clear. By refusing to help IMIA she would be putting her friends at risk. It was a horrendous position to be in.

'Lucas Black was right.' Cate looked down at her hands. 'He told me in Australia that I didn't have any idea what I was mixed up in, that I was way too young to be working for you, and that you should leave me alone. He'd been in the army, in counter-intelligence. He knew what I didn't – that spying isn't something you can dip in and out of when you want. It's a trap and, once you're stuck in it, it's almost impossible to get out.'

Marcus made a sound of protest, but she carried on regardless. 'And my dad knew exactly the things you are capable of doing. That's why he was so mad at you in France – he didn't want his daughter anywhere near you.' She shook her head. 'I've been so dumb. I thought I was clever, but I was dumb.'

'No, Cate!' Marcus said. 'You're one of the brightest, sharpest teenagers I've ever met.' His face softened. 'We have asked an awful lot of you and we still are. But IMIA need to tackle these awful crimes. You've helped to make the world a much safer, better place. How many sixteen-year-olds can say that?'

There was a long silence.

Cate managed a tiny smile. 'It's not exactly something I can put on my university application form though, is it?'

Marcus flashed his toothy grin. 'We just keep an eye on Tyler, try and work out who his contacts are, where he's been recently, who he hangs out with. Oh, and have this.'

He handed her a small metal tin. She opened it to find a couple of tiny listening devices, each with a satellite tail hanging from it like a thread.

'We need one in his car and in his phone,' Marcus said, ignoring her stricken look. 'Once they're in place, you can forget all about it.' He sighed. 'If I didn't think for one minute that you were capable – more than capable – of getting us what we need, I wouldn't ask you. And neither would Henri.'

'Cate,' said Henri, who had been pacing impatiently around the room while Marcus talked, 'face facts. It's your friends and your mother who are somehow caught up in this crime. We have to get to the bottom of it.'

Much as Cate wanted to pretend that the whole thing wasn't happening, she knew that running away from it wasn't going to save her mother from investigation – maybe even arrest – nor would it help the twins.

Henri coughed. 'Look, I'll make a deal with you. If you help us, plant the bugs, get us some information, I promise that, whatever you or we find out, I will do my utmost to protect your mother from the fallout.' He looked her straight in the eye, and this time there was no hostility, just respect and sincerity. 'I give you my word as the head of IMIA.'

The silence in the room seemed to last for ever. Cate sighed. Her mother was flaky, irresponsible and downright daft sometimes, but Cate was sure she wasn't a criminal.

'I'll do it,' she said eventually. 'But you'll keep your promise, won't you?'

'It's a done deal already,' Henri said firmly.

He put his hand out to Cate and, after a few seconds' hesitation, she shook it.

'Welcome back, Cate Carlisle,' said Henri.

'Please be there, Arthur, please answer.' Cate was sitting crosslegged on the bed, her tablet leaning against a stack of pillows while she desperately tried to reach her brother on Skype.

She checked her watch again. It was quite late in London but she knew Arthur would still be up.

'Hey, Cate.' Suddenly his face was on the screen. 'I was expecting you to call much later. I didn't even get to check my new invention! I've just fitted a recognition system in the Skype software to remotely activate my alarm clock if your number rings. I don't want to be woken up by some computer mate in Australia going on about their latest hacking logarithms.'

Cate smiled. Arthur talked like a hardened techie, but right now, with his hair sticking up on end, he looked about ten years old, so cute that she wanted to reach through the screen and cuddle him.

'Arthur, it's so good to see you,' Cate said happily. 'Nice hair, by the way.'

His face creased into a grin as he tried in vain to smooth down his wayward chestnut mop. 'Very funny. Now did you call me to say hello – or have you got something special to tell me? And how's LA? What have you been doing?'

'Where do I begin?' said Cate slowly. 'So much has happened since I arrived. Dad has probably told you already that Mum has been delayed in Mexico and I'm staying in this amazing hotel in Santa Monica.'

'Sure,' said Arthur. 'Isn't Mum hopeless? I googled the hotel though. Looks awesome. I'm dead jealous.'

Cate hesitated. In the aftermath of IMIA's visit, her first thought had been to confide in Arthur and tell him exactly what they had said. But then her protective instinct had kicked in. Arthur was only fourteen and, to Cate, who had comforted Arthur in the dark days following their mother's departure, he was especially precious. She couldn't bring herself to tell him that their mother had got herself mixed up at best with an unsavoury boyfriend, and at worst in criminal activity. And if she wasn't going to do that, she might as well keep quiet about IMIA paying her a visit. For now at least.

'Arthur, you're right, I have got something to tell you. You remember I told you about the twins I met at the turtle sanctuary? They were from California. Good fun, studying archaeology.'

Arthur nodded.

'Well, I've bumped into a friend of theirs here in LA and it appears they've gone missing – from a dig in Mexico, where, rumour has it, they and their friends had just found something very special.'

'Treasure?' asked Arthur eagerly. 'Wow.'

'No one really knows at the moment,' said Cate slowly. 'It seems that whatever they found has vanished as well. There have been other robberies too, all over Mexico.'

'I haven't heard a whiff of this on any of the internet sites,' he mused, 'and I talk to people in Mexico all the time.'

'It's been hushed up,' Cate explained. 'The Mexican government is terrified in case it destroys their tourism industry.'

Arthur shrugged. 'Makes sense. But, Cate, why are we talking about this now?'

'You know that I can never resist a mystery,' Cate began.

'Mmm.'

'And I know the twins. I really want to try and help them. I'm sure half the Mexican government is working on it, but couldn't you and I have a go at trying to find out what's happened to them?'

'What are you like, sis?' Arthur grinned. 'You can't go on holiday and just chill, can you? You have to find something to do – usually crime-related.' He suddenly looked worried. 'This isn't something you're planning on getting really involved with, are you? I don't think I could stand it if you got yourself into danger again like last time – and the time before!'

Cate paused. The last thing she wanted to do was lie to her brother. She thought back to what IMIA had said. They just wanted her to keep an eye on Burt. That was hardly dangerous – not compared to the stuff she had done for them in the past.

'Arthur, I'm in LA – this is all happening in Mexico.' Cate looked her brother right in the eye. 'They're several hundred miles apart. I think I'm pretty safe.'

Arthur relaxed visibly. 'OK, sis, of course I'll help. You know I love a challenge as much as you do and it'll give me a break from exam revision.'

'Thanks,' Cate said, trying hard not to feel guilty. 'You're a legend.'

'So, what's the plan?'

She looked at the list she had scrawled down shortly after the IMIA agents had left the room. 'I'll send you the names of the ancient sites that were hit. See if you can find anything to link them. Maybe there's a reason why these sites were targeted and not others.'

'Sure, no problem.' Arthur was excited now, she could tell. 'I'll try and hack into the Mexican police reports too. See how far they've got and how hard they're looking for your friends. Just one question: How did you know about the attacks on the other sites when it's all been hushed up?'

Cate felt a stab of annoyance at herself, followed swiftly by a warm feeling of pride in her brother's quick-wittedness. Trust Arthur to pick up on that.

'Er, long story,' she said finally. 'Can I tell you later? I'm desperate for a swim and a nice long relax by the pool.'

'OK.' Arthur sounded puzzled but he didn't push it. 'Whenever you're ready. In the meantime, I'll get to work. And say hi to Mum and give her a big hug from me. Exams, huh? They suck. I can't wait till I see her in the summer.'

Sitting on the empty hotel terrace, sipping her Diet Coke and enjoying the mid-afternoon sun, Cate heard her mother coming long before she saw her. First it was the sound of the powerful sports car racing into the Erin car park and screeching to a resounding halt right outside reception, then she heard the clack of high heels on the floor as her mother made her entrance.

'Darling,' she called as she raced towards her daughter, her arms outstretched. 'How amazing to see you.'

Cate was enveloped in a huge, bony embrace, and she smelled expensive perfume, lipstick, and her leather gilet.

She and her mum Skyped regularly, but it was so different to be face to face. She had forgotten how thin her mother was, how birdlike, and Cate realised that she was now a head taller than her. After a few moments her mother pulled away and, lifting up her oversized Gucci sunglasses, held Cate at arm's length, studying her face.

'Oh my God,' she said. 'You've grown up. You grew up when I wasn't looking and now my baby is gone for ever.'

To her horror, Cate could see tears in her mother's huge green eyes. She too, was on the verge of crying. Instead she smiled and reached out for her mother's hands, giving them a little shake.

'It's OK, Mum,' she said. 'Don't get upset. I'm doing fine and so's Arthur. We're really happy. Dad's great and Monique's cool.'

She pulled her mother down on to one of the wicker seats next to her and did her best to keep the mood light-hearted.

'Mum, isn't this place wonderful? You should see my room. It's got a juicer and a huge balcony. It's even got a mixer desk. Fancy a go?'

Her mother's still-flawless English-rose skin was tight over her razor-sharp cheekbones. She looked nearer to Cate's age than her own, Cate thought.

'I can't get over how much you look like your father,' said her mother. 'In a good way, of course. Is he still spending more time worrying about the problems of the world than he does about his own family?'

'Mum!' Cate protested. The last thing she wanted was for her mother to start her usual sniping about her father.

'Sorry, darling,' said her mother, sounding not at all sorry. She looked around for a waiter. 'Any chance of a drink? We had a hellish journey from Mexico. First we waited ten hours for this contact of Burt's to turn up with this amazingly cheap stock and then he didn't even show up! I was furious with Burt, especially when he admitted he'd never even met the man and had no real idea who he was.

IMIA again, thought Cate grimly. Up to their usual tricks.

'And then, coming back,' her mother continued, 'two tyres on that wretched hired van blew at the same time, just as we left San Diego.' She shook her head. 'I was beginning to think I was jinxed. I was desperate, just desperate, to get back to see you. I do miss you, Cate. It's not so bad when you're on the other side of the world, but knowing you were so close, it was torture not to be able to see you.'

'Never mind, you're here now. That's all that matters.' Cate squeezed her mother's hand. In spite of everything, she did still adore her.

'Where's Burt?' she asked her mother casually.

'He's gone straight to the shop to see if there was anything taken by those men you saw.'

Cate had told her mum about the men at the shop but left out the bunker bit. She hadn't wanted her to panic.

'In fact, since we got your call he's been like a cat on a hot tin roof, desperate to get back and check on the shop, see if anything had been taken or damaged,' her mother carried on. 'I honestly thought he was going to get us arrested for speeding the way he was driving. And to top it all, apparently his pick-up truck has been stolen too and used in some kind of road rage incident and is in a bad way. Luckily, he can collect that in the next few days. He nearly had a fit when the police said they needed to hold on to it for forensics.'

Cate hoped that her expression wasn't giving her away. She

hadn't told her mother about being driven off the road either – she didn't think she could bear the inevitable fuss.

Her mother yawned, covering her teeth with her neatly manicured fingers. 'To be honest, darling, it's all a bit much for me. I leave the business side to Burt. I'm the front woman, good at chatting to the customers, networking, PR, that sort of thing.'

'So where do you get most of your stuff? Is it really old?' Cate asked casually.

Her mother gave a tinkling laugh as she waved at Rosie. 'Oh no, darling. Well, sort of old-new, if you know what I mean. Most of it comes from factories in Mexico and is distressed to make it look authentic. You know, roughed up, dirtied, given the odd coat of wash, a little bit of Mexican scribble here and there. Then we don't exactly say it's old but we don't say it's new either. We just call it authentic Mexican art and double the price.'

Cate's eyebrows shot up.

'Oh darling, don't be so po-faced. It's what everyone in retail does. It's all about perception.'

Rosie was standing next to them now, looking down politely at Cate's mother.

'I'll have a large gin and tonic with lime,' she said, looking with obvious interest at Rosie's lurid nail art. 'And my daughter will have . . . ?'

'An orange juice and soda, please. With lots of ice,' Cate replied, not looking at Rosie.

'No problem,' said Rosie amiably. 'Be with you in a minute.'

Two young women clad in matching red swimming costumes and tiny denim shorts strutted confidently on to the beach in front of where they were sitting, long hair bouncing down their perfectly honed and tanned backs. Behind them their boyfriends, all bulging biceps and narrow hips, were carrying surfboards on their shoulders.

Cate's mother looked down at her lean, narrow thighs and sighed. 'Honestly, Cate, it's so tough being constantly surrounded with perfection. Even Burt's better looking than me. I'm always wondering if I should lose another few pounds, have some more botox, get some hair extensions . . .'

'You look pretty stunning to me,' said Cate loyally. She meant it. Her mother was amazing, especially for her age. 'People will think we're sisters, not mother and daughter.'

'You think so?' Cate's mother brightened up immediately. 'Oh darling, how sweet of you to say so. I tell you what. How about we go shopping together tomorrow? Have a lovely girlie day at the mall and get our nails done. I'll take you to Third Street – it's amazing. All the celebs go there to shop. The new Market Place Mall looks like something from outer space. There's a Bloomingdale's and Swarovski and Juicy Couture, and I'll treat you to a pair of jeans at Seven For All Mankind. And then we'll have a fabulous lunch at the taco bar. How does that sound?'

Rosie arrived with the iced drinks.

'It sounds great, Mum,' Cate said, picking her drink up. 'I can't think of anything better than spending a day mooching around the shops with you. It's something we never get the chance to do.'

'It's a date,' said her mother, patting her on the hand. She sucked at her drink thoughtfully. 'Cate, you know what you said about us looking like sisters?'

Cate nodded warily.

'Well, perhaps you shouldn't be calling me "Mum" any more. Perhaps now you're practically grown up you should start using my real name. After all . . .' She winked at her daughter conspiratorially. '. . . We don't want people thinking I was a teenage mother, now do we?'

Cate stared aghast at her mother. Of all the things she had steeled herself to accept about her mother's lack of maternal instincts, this couldn't be one of them. She shook her head slowly. 'Sorry,' she said, 'I've not had much chance to use the word "Mum" and I'm not ready to stop yet.'

There was an uncomfortable silence and Cate was grateful when her phone rang in her bag.

'Nancy!' Cate had forgotten to call her about dinner. 'Sorry, Nancy, my mum was delayed. I haven't had a chance to ask her about dinner. Just a minute.' Cate put her hand over the phone. 'Um, it's my friend Nancy Kyle. She wondered if we'd like to join her and her boyfriend Lucas for dinner tonight? You OK with that?'

'*The* Nancy Kyle?' whispered Cate's mother, her eyes gleaming. She flapped her hand at her daughter. 'Well, say yes, darling, of course. Of course we'll be there.'

'Er, yeah, Nancy. Mum says thanks, that'd be great. You'll pick us up? Wicked. At eight. OK. See you then.'

She put her phone back in her bag. 'She's suggesting a pop-up restaurant somewhere along the coast. Sorry, Mum, I should have said earlier. I saw Nancy last night and she was keen for us to go out – me, you, Lucas and her.'

But not Burt. Cate really didn't want to have to spend the evening with a man she hadn't even met. Particularly one who might be a criminal.

'Oh, that's wonderful, darling.' Her mother was clearly too excited to either notice or care that Burt had been left off the guest list. 'I love Nancy Kyle. She's so elegant. And that boyfriend of hers – such a talented songwriter. I had no idea you knew her. How on earth did you meet?'

'In the South of France,' Cate said, trying not to show how pleased she was that her mum was so impressed. 'You remember my summer job – on the yacht? Well, it turned out to be Nancy's yacht and I helped to look after her five children. We've stayed in touch ever since.'

'Fantastic,' breathed her mother. 'Well, there's no time to go back to my place. The traffic is terrible at this time of day. Come on, darling. Let's head up to your room and raid your suitcase. After all, we are practically the same size.' She looked Cate up and down. 'Although you're probably just a smidgeon heavier than me now, darling, don't you think?'

CHAPTER 10

The black limousine glided gracefully along the tarmac that led from the highway down to the ocean's edge.

'Where are we going, honey?' Nancy leaned across the walnut table and gave Lucas's hand a squeeze. 'This is the right place, yeah? I've got my new Jimmy Choos on, after all. I had to wait a whole three months for them to come in at Bloomingdale's and I don't want to wreck them the first time I take them out.'

Lucas rolled his eyes at his girlfriend. 'Don't worry, Nancy. Your Choos are safe with me,' he said. 'Two more minutes, tops. I promise you, this place is well worth the journey. Pete the drummer went to the last pop-up this chef organised. He said it was the coolest night he had ever had in LA. And that's saying something.' He paused for effect then turned to Cate, who was sitting next to him. 'He sends his love to you, by the way.'

Cate felt herself going pink, remembering how Pete had teased her when she had travelled with Black Noir last Christmas, pretending to ask her on a date.

Nancy homed in on her embarrassment. 'Speaking of boyfriends, Cate,' she said, 'that Ritchie seems like rather a catch. Nephew of Johnny James, no less. I should hang in there if I were you.'

Cate's mother's eyebrows shot up and she stared at her daughter.

'But,' Nancy continued, warming to her theme, 'your lovely Michel was utterly gorgeous and a real sweetheart. He played the saxophone like an angel. And he was French. What's not to like? *Très romantique*.'

'Chip off the old block, darling, chip off the old block,' said Cate's mother, giving Cate an approving look. 'I was exactly the same at your age.'

Cate pulled a face at them both and looked out of the window. In the glass reflection she saw Lucas wink at her and she grinned back, reluctantly at first and then with genuine warmth.

It's only a bit of teasing, she thought. In truth, Cate had been terrified that Nancy and her mother wouldn't get on. Both of them were extremely competitive around other – particularly pretty – women. Yet they had bonded like sisters, chatting non-stop all the way from Santa Monica, comparing gossip on the wacky diets of various female celebrities, the latest botox techniques and the coolest places to shop in LA.

Meanwhile, Cate was enthralled as Lucas told her about his Mexican documentary and the trip to Mexico City that had inspired it.

'It was life-changing,' Lucas said, 'to see all those kids sleeping in sewers, out on the streets desperately trying to sell bits of thrown-away tat that they had picked out of bins or from tips.' He shook his head, his dark eyes sad. 'Kids of seven or eight trying to look after toddlers. Fighting over filthy rags just so that they could lie down and get a few hours' sleep. It just beggars belief. Here in the twenty-first century, in a relatively wealthy country, just over the border from the richest state in America, kids are living like that. I knew there and then I had to do anything I could to help them.'

'What you're doing is amazing,' Cate said. 'One concert from you and one fashion show from Nancy will raise more awareness and money than all the politicians in the world put together.'

'Thanks, Cate,' said Lucas softly. 'That means a lot.'

The car rounded a bend and suddenly Cate saw dozens of dancing, flickering lights up ahead. As her eyes adjusted, she saw there were fairy lights strung along the edge of a marina. Behind them, the small bright lights from the masts of yachts rose and fell with the gentle ocean swell and, up ahead, Cate could see the outline of a large marquee, the front side lifted up to reveal candlelit tables and chairs facing out towards the huge boats.

The limousine slid noiselessly to a halt just in front of the marquee and a uniformed waiter, with film-star looks, rushed to open the door. Cate got out on to a thick red carpet, where she stood still for a few seconds, revelling in the feeling of the warm Pacific breeze caressing her face. She was joined by Lucas, then her mother, and the three of them stood there for a few seconds, blinking as their eyes adjusted to the bright lights.

From the marquee Cate heard the clink of wine glasses, some jazz music playing softly, and people laughing. This was going to be an amazing evening, she thought happily to herself. Not bad for only her second evening in LA!

Suddenly the maitre d' was rushing towards them, his arms opened in welcome. 'Mr Black, what an honour to see you. Thank you for coming.' He shook Lucas's outstretched hand, then turned to Cate and her mother. 'And your two beautiful companions. *Bonjour*, welcome, welcome. I hope you will stay for the dancing later?'

Behind him, a short man with slicked-back hair was advancing towards them with a purposeful look on his face.

'My photographer.' The maitre d' gestured towards him apologetically. 'If you would be so good as to have your photograph taken? Such wonderful publicity for my pop-up restaurant would be immeasurable. I would be so grateful.'

Cate felt Lucas hesitating, then he smiled. 'No problem, François. You know I think you are doing a fantastic thing. I love pop-ups. They give the unrecognised chefs a chance to make a name for themselves without the cost of opening a restaurant.'

Lucas put his arms around the two women obligingly and the photographer clicked away on his camera whilst François beamed with pride. So this must be what it feels like to be famous, thought Cate, grinning happily. What if the pictures somehow found their way to the UK, maybe even into the celebrity magazines her friends read with such devotion? That would be beyond awesome.

The photographer was still clicking away when Cate heard François gasp. Nancy Kyle, her bright red lipstick newly applied, her huge green eyes accentuated by her kohl make-up, was out of the car.

Without waiting for Lucas, she strode up the red carpet on impossibly high stilettos, her shapely hips swaying as if she were on a catwalk, her white jumpsuit shimmering under the coloured lights, her impossibly tiny waist cinched in by a wide snakeskin-effect belt.

Instantly the cameraman forgot about Lucas, Cate and her mother and started taking pictures of a seemingly oblivious Nancy, who by now was making her entrance into the marquee.

Lucas grinned at Cate. 'Oh, that poor Nancy, I do worry about her,' he said sardonically, exaggerating his flat Northern vowels. 'She is so shy and retiring.' He took Cate's mother on one arm and offered the other to Cate. 'Come on, guys, let's go follow the star.'

By the time Cate had worked her way through the fourth course of the tasting menu, she was ready to call it a day. She had already eaten tiny, precise squares of venison saddle perched on a risotto base, a triangle of salmon poached in a liquorice gel, jelly of quail presented in a silver egg cup, and she had even shut her eyes and tried a teaspoon of snail porridge. Despite their small size, the portions had been surprisingly filling.

Cate looked around with interest. Some of the fellow diners looked very familiar indeed. Tucked away discreetly in the corner she saw a famous golfer, recently divorced after a scandalous affair, topping up the champagne glass of a giggling peroxide blonde. On the table next to them, the man behind the biggest reality TV franchise in the world was locked in earnest conversation with three men in grey suits and, on the other side of the marquee, a famously bad-tempered TV chef was clearly checking out the opposition.

Cate tried hard not to gape. For a pop-up restaurant, this place certainly brought out the stars.

Her mum caught her eye and gave her a wink. 'Look behind you,' she whispered. 'Just come in.'

Cate turned in what she hoped was a casual movement and then nearly fell from her chair. On the very next table, Jake Breber, the boy pop wonder of the year, was playing on a tablet. His unmistakable dark fringe was swept immaculately across his boyish face, his famous smile contorted into a grimace as he hit the controls in a frenzy. Next to him, almost dwarfing the diminutive teenager, a huge man with cropped iron-grey hair scanned the room with a suspicious expression, his hand holding what looked like a tiny microphone. Jake Breber certainly wasn't Cate's favourite singer. In fact, his lovelorn lyrics and sugary melodies made Cate want to throw her radio out of the window every time they were played. But she knew she was in the minority amongst her friends.

Nancy put down her glass and nudged Lucas. 'It's that Jake Breber,' she whispered so loudly that Cate cringed, certain that the boy wonder must have heard her. 'You should get him to play at your gig next week, Lucas,' Nancy continued brightly. 'Perhaps he could duet with you on your charity download. He'd get all the teenagers digging deep to help your Mexican street kids.'

'Nancy, Black Noir are bona fide musicians,' he said patiently. 'We are not a boy band. We're properly trained musically, with years of hard slog on the tour circuit behind us and fans who actually know something about our genre. If we go on stage with Jake, well, let's just say that you and I might not be flying by private jet this time next year. So let's leave young Master Breber to the teenyboppers' singalong, shall we?'

'Harsh, Lucas,' said Nancy. 'You were young once.'

He raised his eyebrows at her.

They did like needling each other, Cate thought. Perhaps that was what they had in common. Apart from money and fame, sometimes she really couldn't see what else kept them together.

CHAPTER 11

'I'm just off to the bathroom,' said Cate. She picked up her bag and followed the signs to a series of plush portable loos located outside, close to the boats. As she picked her way across the boardwalk, she heard the metal stays clanking against the steel masts – a sound that always reminded Cate of her time working on Nancy's yacht.

She headed back to the marquee and then stopped and looked towards the marina. She adored looking at yachts, fantasising about which one she would buy if she ever won the lottery or, more likely, if Arthur became a nerdy billionaire. No, she couldn't resist a quick sightseeing detour.

As Cate walked towards the boats, she heard the deep-throated rumble of a yacht coming into the marina. She peered through the gloom and saw it. It was around ten metres long and nosing gently into a mooring on the pontoon directly in front.

Onboard, a crowd of young people were milling around, passing ropes, laughing and shouting good-natured instructions to one another. Their voices were carrying clearly over the water. The boat safely moored, they piled out on to the pontoon, ten or so of them, the boys resplendent in black tie, the girls in cocktail dresses. They passed close by Cate in a waft of perfume and expensive aftershave, looking as if they had stepped from a Ralph Lauren advertisement.

Not a bad way to spend a Saturday night, thought Cate. 'Jump on a yacht and head off to a pop-up restaurant somewhere along the coast for dinner and dancing. Kids their age in England would be probably falling out of pubs in the rain, jumping on to grubby buses or waiting ages for a grumpy taxi driver to deign to stop for them.

Cate was distracted from her thoughts by the sight of a man up ahead. He was carrying a thick package under his left arm and heading down to the boats. Even from that distance, there was something about him – his height, the shape of his head – that looked familiar. Intrigued, she stepped down on to the wooden pontoon that edged the marina and began to walk slowly towards him. It was darker down there, the overhead lights of the restaurant beginning to fade, the only illumination the mast lights far above her.

Then Cate saw the man's pale face and icy blue eyes and instinctively she stepped back into the shadows. There, less than twenty metres away, was Novak, Johnny James's head of security. Wasn't he meant to be in New York?

She shook her head. What Novak did in his time off was no business of hers. But as the tall man headed away from her she noticed he was limping badly, and as he passed a lit-up boat she saw that his right arm was folded, useless, against his chest. Now Cate was intrigued. She wondered who or what had given Novak those injuries.

Almost without thinking, she was following him, slipping

113

off her shoes and feeling the coolness of the wooden boards beneath her feet. Below her the water sucked and sighed, the boards vibrating with her weight as she walked. She chose her route carefully, keeping close to the yachts, using their large frames as a cover as she kept a safe distance from her target.

It was just as well that she was being so cautious. Novak was clearly worried about being followed, turning suddenly every twenty metres or so, once or twice disappearing into the shadows only to reappear after a short wait.

The longer Cate followed him, the more she was convinced that he was up to no good. She hesitated and pulled back into the shadows. Back at the restaurant they would soon be missing her, sending her a text, then perhaps even coming out to look for her. She had to stall them. She texted her mother.

Back in five. Just chatting to someone.

Enough, she hoped, to buy her some time. She put the phone on to silent and carried on after him.

Novak reached a T-junction in the walkway and veered off to the left, heading out across the marina, to where the larger, deepwater boats were moored.

He was moving more slowly now, looking up at the side of the yachts, clearly hoping to see a name – and finally it seemed he had found the right boat. He gave a careful glance over both shoulders before climbing on to the wooden gangplank at the rear of a black motor yacht that stood three storeys high, lights blazing in the dark.

Ming Yue. Registered Hong Kong.

The name was inscribed in gothic gold script on the side of the boat, just below a brass railing which glowed like a halo. The glass doors were not quite pulled shut and Cate could hear the murmur of men's voices. She looked at the short walkway that was hanging temptingly between the pontoon and the boat, and tiptoed quietly on to the outer deck. She stood there for a few seconds, listening out for any signs that she had been heard, but the voices continued unabated.

Gently, quietly, she moved in close enough to look through the large glass doors that led through to the main cabin. The blinds had been pulled down but they weren't completely closed so she could peer through and see inside.

Novak was sitting with his back to her in a leather captain's chair, his pale scalp gleaming through his closely shaven hair, his good elbow leaning on a wooden table. He was partially blocking her view of the man opposite, but she could see enough to recognise that he was Chinese, oldish, with greying hair and a thickset body.

The two men were poring over photographs but, try as she might, Cate couldn't see any detail, nor could she hear what they were discussing. She grimaced in frustration, then remembered her iPhone. It might just work. She reached into her pocket and clicked on to the camera. She held the phone up to the crack in the window and pressed first the film and then the zoom button.

She had to stop herself from gasping in surprise. All the photographs were of what seemed to her to be Mexican antiquities, made from gold and silver, studded with semi-precious stones – death masks, necklaces, bracelets – all in high definition colour.

She was just about to press the record button when she heard a sniffing around her ankles and felt a wet sensation on her bare feet. She looked down at a tiny rough-haired terrier on a lead. Stifling a yelp of shock, she instinctively pulled her foot away. The little dog bared his teeth in response and began to bark loudly.

'What's that, Zan?' The Chinese man looked up sharply from

his chair and Cate sank back behind the blinds, praying that the darkness would protect her from being seen.

Cate reached out to stroke the dog in a desperate attempt to placate it, but it growled and then broke into a bark again. This time the Chinese man stood up and Cate saw Novak turning around stiffly in his chair.

It was time to make a quick escape. Cate shoved her phone into her pocket, picked up her shoes and ran softly down the gangplank, the dog still yapping behind her. For a few terrible seconds she thought it would follow her, but it stopped just short of the bridge, its tail wagging furiously as the two men came out on the deck and peered out at the pontoon. She froze, hidden in the shadow of the boat.

'Zan, Zan, hush. Who's there?' The Chinese man sounded angry, annoyed and the look of menace on Novak's face left Cate in no doubt about how she would be treated if they spotted her.

After what seemed like hours, the two men finally turned to go back into the cabin. Cate was just about to slip out of the shadows when she heard a rasping bark and saw the dog running out on to the gangway. It had obviously been let off its lead. Any time now, Cate thought, it would bring the men right to her.

She frantically checked through her options. If she made a bolt for it, she knew they would catch her in an instant. She couldn't get up on to the other boats – their vast hulls were slippery and impossible to climb up without at least a rope.

Her eyes fell on a small metal box, just a few metres to her left. She recognised instantly what it was. When she had been working on Nancy's yacht, one of her first jobs when they docked was to go on to the gangway and plug the yacht in to the marina's power supply.

She crept quietly over to the box, feeling for the thick plug which fed into the mains supply and tugged on it hard, yanking it out of its socket. A split-second later, the entire pontoon was in total darkness and Cate was running like the wind, back to the safety of the restaurant.

'Pudding, Cate?' asked Lucas, as she slipped back quietly into her seat, hoping that no one would notice her still-flushed face and rushed breathing.

A large plate of miniature desserts had just arrived at the table, each one as pretty as a cupcake, and her mother and Nancy were cooing over them like excited schoolgirls. Her fears that she might be missed seemed to have been unfounded. Nancy was showing Cate's mother a copy of *Vogue* with her on the cover and the pair of them were discussing just how stunning the supermodel was looking in a shoot for faux furs.

Poor Lucas, thought Cate. He must have been bored.

'I might model one at the charity fashion show,' Nancy said thoughtfully. 'They make me look, well, so classy.'

'Speaking of the charity,' Lucas wiped his mouth with a pure white damask napkin, 'the documentary we're going to play at the fashion show needs to be a real tear-jerker, to explain just why this fundraiser is so important, why people have to dig deep. Me and the band have decided that we need more footage on the street kids themselves. So we'll be flying down to Veracruz, probably the day after tomorrow. We'll be there for a few days while we shoot a few more scenes. Have you got time to come, Nancy? You could even be in the shoot. It makes sense. It's your fashion show, after all.'

Nancy pursed her lips. 'Weeell,' she said finally, 'as long as I'm back in time to get my dress fitted and my hair done for the weekend. What about you, Cate?'

'Me?' Cate said surprised. 'You want me to come to Mexico?'

'Why not? You can keep me company. These shoots are sooo boring. Lucas disappears for hours at a time and when he gets back all he wants to do is sleep.'

Cate's mind did a quick scan back over the map of Mexico that Marcus had shown her that morning.

'Did you say Veracruz?' she said, trying very hard to make it sound like a throwaway question. 'Isn't that near to El Tajin?'

'Very near,' said Lucas, 'but it's not the best known of the archaeological sites in Mexico. I'm surprised you've heard of it.'

'We did a Mexican history project at school,' said Cate, not meeting his eye. She hated lying, especially to someone like Lucas who had shown her nothing but kindness. 'I've always wanted to go there. But Mum and I have only just got together. I can't just whizz off.'

'Oh, Ronnie, you must come too,' Nancy said casually. 'You're my new best friend. There's a fab hotel in Veracruz. Infinity pools, spa, moonlit yoga, the most divine massage. My treat of course.'

Cate's mum beamed around the table. 'Well,' she said, 'if you put it like that. Of course, I'd be delighted to join you. Cate, let's go to Mexico!'

'Darling, whatever happened to your shoes?' her mother said as they made themselves comfortable in the limousine for the return journey to the Erin.

Cate looked down at her feet and winced. That wretched dog must have been quietly chewing at her left shoe before it decided to lick her foot. The wooden buttons at the front were completely gone. She suddenly felt sick. She doubted the dog would have swallowed them, which meant that they were still back on the boat. So now Novak and his friend would know for sure that someone had been on that boat tonight.

She just had to hope that they would never find out that it had been her.

Cate's mother's house lay high in the Hollywood Hills at the end of a steep, winding road lined with bright pink bougainvillea and purple hibiscus flowers, which contrasted sharply with the harsh scrubland and dusty tarmac roads.

Cate and her mother had both stayed at the hotel for the night. It was still early in the morning when they set out; the dew had not yet dried on the bright-green lawns in front of the white villas and apartment blocks that clung to the hillside with grim determination. The pine-scented air was sharp and clean, the sky a bright blue, not yet tainted by the LA smog.

'Here we are,' said Cate's mother as the sports car turned sharply into an almost-vertical driveway and came to a halt in front of a large white archway. Cate had been too distracted by her mother's crazy driving on the way up to look at the view, but now, as she got out of the car, she found herself gasping in amazement at what lay before her.

Down in the valley below was the city of LA, a vast urban sprawl that stretched up and down the coast almost as far as the eye could see. Cate could just make out the highway running inland from the golden beaches and huge endless ocean.

To her right, she spotted the famous Hollywood sign, and behind it the Santa Monica mountains rose up, menacing yet beautiful with their lilac-pink bodies topped with glistening white snow.

Cate followed her mother through the archway and round to the back of the house. The garden had been dug into the hillside, with a lawn and terraced steps. On the first level, immediately in front of the house, lay a small kidney-shaped swimming pool, edged by dark red tiles on which large terracotta pots full of tumbling flowers were placed at regular intervals.

'It's gorgeous,' said Cate, as she drank in the bright colours and felt the promise of warm sunshine on her face.

Cate's mother pushed open the large glass doors and, reaching inside, punched some numbers into the burglar alarm. To her own bemusement, Cate felt herself automatically watching her mother's finger and memorising the numbers. Two – eight – zero – six. Arthur's birthday. She wondered if that had been by accident or design.

The ground floor was open plan, a wide staircase coming up from the middle of the floor to a galleried area above her. Cate's room was at the end of the gallery, a small en-suite with a large window, which to her delight looked out on to the city below them.

'It's really pretty at night,' said her mother as she helped Cate to unpack. 'All the lights twinkling in front of you, up and down the hillside. Sometimes it feels as if you're in the middle of the galaxy. Perhaps if you came to live with me, then you might get to know and love LA as much as I do.'

Cate shot her a questioning glance. It was the first time her mother had ever mentioned anything about them living together.

'You could think about coming to uni here,' she continued. 'UCLA has a great reputation for science.'

As always, when she and her mother began to talk about anything remotely to do with their relationship, Cate felt tongue-tied, unable to say what she really wanted to for fear of provoking tears from either her mother or herself.

'My teachers want me to try for Oxbridge,' said Cate, eventually. 'but I'll certainly think about it.'

The subsequent silence was broken by the sound of a car pulling into the drive below them. Cate's mother looked out of the window and smiled.

'Burt,' she said brightly. 'He's early. We'll be down in a minute, darling,' she trilled out of the window as a dark-haired muscular-looking man jumped out of a bright-red hatchback. Even from that distance, Cate could see he was agitated, sweating profusely, pulling at the bag on his front seat in jerky movements. He slammed the door shut and the car shook. Beside her, Cate's mother winced.

'Cate's here,' she said, waving. 'She's just dying to meet you.'

CHAPTER 12

'Arthur, I have just sat through the worst lunch of my life – ever.' Cate was up in the bedroom Skyping Arthur who was patiently listening to his sister's rantings. 'And I'm not talking about the food.'

'Well, what's he like?' Arthur got straight to the point. 'Better or worse than the yacht captain? Or the yoga instructor? Or the Kabala preacher? Has he got smelly breath? BO? A shocking beard?'

'Arthur!' Cate tried to sound outraged, but was too busy laughing. No matter how serious the situation, Arthur always managed to find the humour in it.

'Actually I suppose he's really good looking if you like that buffed Hollywood actor type. He's a lot younger than Mum I'd say, only just forty, and he looks like he works out. But boy was he tense. He was sweating the whole time and kept snarling at Mum when she asked him if he'd had a good morning. He hardly even glanced at me, let alone spoke to me.'

'Perhaps he was upset you were there,' ventured Arthur. 'Jealous, maybe?'

'Maybe,' said Cate doubtfully, 'but I got the impression it wasn't personal. Every time a car drove past the house, he kept looking up; and when the patio door slammed, he jumped up as if he'd been shot. Hang on a second.' She went to the window and came back a moment later.

'Sorry, Arthur,' she said, settling down on the bed again. 'Just checking the coast is clear. It's OK, Mum's downstairs by the pool with Burt. I'd hate her to overhear. By the way, have you scrambled the Skype signal so no one can listen in?'

'Of course.' Arthur sounded slightly offended. 'Do you even have to ask? Every single computer in the house – and that includes laptops, tablets and phones – has been given the same treatment. Bill Gates himself couldn't crack my safety features.'

'Cheers, Arthur. Just checking.'

'No problem,' said her brother cheerfully. 'Anyway, apart from the weird boyfriend, what's up? I've got nothing yet on those ancient sites you told me about. Even computer geeks need to sleep sometimes, you know.'

'Really?' joked Cate. 'I thought you were up all night, like badgers and owls.'

'Actually,' Arthur corrected her, 'that's a myth. Owls hunt in the day as well as at night.'

'Sorry,' said Cate. 'I stand corrected. Anyway, Arthur . . .' She was suddenly serious. 'I need to tell you something. Fess up, really.'

She had been dreading this moment, when she had to tell Arthur that she was working with IMIA again. She had hoped to keep it from him, but now, after last night's episode, things had suddenly got more serious. She'd already sent a text to Marcus telling him what she had seen at the marina, and she had a gut feeling that IMIA were going to want more from her than just keeping an eye on Burt. If that was the case, she couldn't keep Arthur in the dark any longer. For a start, she knew she could rely on him more than anyone to find out things that could make or break a case. And apart from the practicalities, it was great to have someone to talk to, to confide in when things got rough, someone who was always on her side.

The last time she had worked for IMIA she had been lucky to escape with her life and, when she had returned from Australia, Arthur had made her promise that if the organisation ever contacted her again, she would simply walk away. How was he going to take the news that she had broken her promise?

'The thing is, Arthur,' she began slowly, 'I don't quite know how to tell you, but IMIA are involved with this . . .'

Cate couldn't bear to see Arthur's face as he digested the news. She shut her eyes and waited for the inevitable explosion.

After a few seconds' silence she opened them again. Arthur was chewing on a cereal bar and looking remarkably calm.

'Well,' said Cate, 'go on, Arthur. Say something. I know you're going to be mad.'

He shook his head. 'It's OK, sis,' he said through a mouthful of food. 'I kind of knew this was going to happen again. IMIA think you're the bee's knees, and you're about as likely to give up on adventures as I am to sell my computers and buy a subscription to the National Trust.'

Cate giggled. 'So you forgive me?' she said, flicking away a rather large fly that had landed on her thigh. 'Thanks, Arthur. And you promise not to tell Dad any of this?'

'Naturally,' said Arthur gravely. 'If you promise not to tell him that I've been hacking again. Even if it is on your behalf. I promised I'd give it up for Lent.'

'It's a deal,' Cate laughed. 'Honestly, Arthur, we're so bad. I can't think where we get it from.' She thought for a moment. 'Each other probably.'

Cate put her bag down on the spare lounger at the side of the pool and tried to avoid the sight of Burt lying asleep on a green lilo, his muscular torso clad only in the tightest pair of Speedos she had ever seen. He had obviously calmed down since lunchtime. Perhaps he had simply been hungry.

She glanced over at her mother. She appeared to be asleep too, but as Cate stuck her toe into the warm turquoise water, she opened her eyes and sat up.

'Hello, darling, where have you been?' she said brightly. 'Do you still want to go shopping this afternoon? We can buy something special for our trip to Mexico.'

Cate looked at the text she'd just received from Marcus. As she guessed, he wanted to meet. Today. Right now.

'It's OK. I'm fine for clothes, really I am.'

Her mother stared at Cate in amazement. 'I find I can always do with more clothes.' She shrugged. 'OK, if you say so. Well, how about a trip to the nail bar? Or the hairdresser's? If you don't mind me saying, sweetie, your grooming is – well, a little British.'

Cate looked at her mother, noting her extraordinarily long, thick hair and her French-polished nails, and bit her lip.

'Thanks, Mum, but I actually wanted to meet someone this afternoon. A friend.'

'Really,' drawled her mother. 'A friend of the male variety, I expect?'

'Yes,' said Cate. After all that wasn't a fib. Marcus was male. 'It won't be for long,' she said hurriedly. 'He's sent me a text. It's just that with me going off to Mexico I thought I would catch up with him and make arrangements for when I got back.'

'It's that boy Nancy mentioned, isn't it? Greg? Ritchie? The nephew of Johnny James.' Her mother sounded amused, intrigued even. 'I have to hand it to you, Cate, you're a fast worker. You're hardly in the country five minutes and you've already bagged yourself an eligible bachelor.'

'It must be all that British grooming,' said Cate, with an innocent look on her face. 'So it's OK if I go? I said I'd meet him at the pier. Is there any chance that you could run me down there, please? Or maybe Burt?' She tried not to wince as she spoke. The last thing she wanted was to share a car with her mother's boyfriend, but she was aware of the bugs that were burning a hole in her rucksack. She wanted rid of them – and fast.

'Good idea. Burt, wake up.'

'What?' He sat up suddenly, nearly dislodging himself from the lilo in the process.

'Burt, can you run Cate into Santa Monica? It will give you two a chance to get to know each other.'

'No problem,' he said, as he pulled himself out of the pool, his black hair slicked back from his face highlighting his razor sharp cheekbones, his perfectly white teeth gleaming against his tanned face. 'I've got a bit of business in town, anyway. I probably won't be back until late, so don't wait up.' He slung a towel around his shoulders and gave Cate's mother a kiss.

'More business?' Cate's mother laughed. 'You are such a busy man nowadays.'

Burt pulled back his lips into a semblance of a smile. 'Hey honey, things are pretty stacked right now,' he said placatingly. 'I've still got to sort out that goddamn mess with the pick-up and we haven't unloaded the stock we brought back from Mexico.

Don't you worry though, honey.' He gave her hand a squeeze. 'Just leave everything to me.'

Fifteen minutes later, Cate was hanging on to the front seat of the red Mustang, hurtling back down the winding road. It wasn't a pleasant experience. Even the freezing-cold air conditioning couldn't remove the faint whiff of sweat and sickly smell of stale aftershave, and Cate could feel the waves of tension coming from the driver. It was all Cate could do not to beg Burt to stop the car and let her out. Instead, she forced herself to concentrate on the task in hand.

'So, Burt,' she said, turning to him. 'How long have you been dealing in Mexican stuff?'

'Not long as it happens,' he said, giving her a sideways glance. 'I used to box, act, do a bit of stunt work and, when that got too painful, I played in a band. After a few years I got a bit too old to be a rock-and-roller.' He grinned self-deprecatingly. 'That was tough. I was washed up, with nothing to do. So I took on removals and house clearances for an old buddy who had a second-hand shop selling furniture and then I went out on my own and got a lock-up in Santa Monica.'

He yanked the car violently around a hairpin bend, narrowly missing a woman who was hanging on to the leads of what seemed like a dozen dogs. As he glared back at her over his shoulder, Cate slipped her right hand down the back of Burt's seat and released the listening device. That was the easy one. She eyed his phone, lying on the tray in between their two seats.

Burt growled as he straightened up the car again. 'Where was I? Oh yeah. Then I bumped into this guy in a hotel – an old friend back from my boxing days. He asked me to help ship some stuff over the border for him from Mexico – you can buy imitation stuff down in Mexico cheaply and bring it here for people to buy at inflated prices. It was good work – easy and the money was great.'

He went quiet and looked again in the rear-view mirror. Something was bothering him, Cate thought.

'After a while I started to bring my own stuff back,' he continued. 'Bits and pieces at first, and then I went the whole hog and rented Mexicano Magic – started selling it myself. That's where your mom comes in.' He grinned mirthlessly at Cate. 'She's got that cool British accent which makes people think they're dealing with some sort of aristocracy. It makes it all more – how shall I say? – respectable.'

Cate stared back at him coldly. 'You mean you flog fakes to innocent people?' She couldn't help herself.

'Hey there! That's harsh.' Burt hit the brakes for a set of traffic lights just as they turned red. 'It's called commerce, Cate. It makes the world go round. Especially here in the good old US of A.'

Cate persevered. 'And do you ever sell – well, anything a bit more precious or genuine?'

Burt shot her a speculative look. 'You kinda nosy, ain't cha?' he said. He had tensed up again and his voice had lost its friendly tone. 'What makes you ask that?'

'No reason.' Cate shrugged, doing her best to look innocent. 'It's just that I love Mexican jewellery. The turquoise stuff.'

'OK. That kind of precious.' Burt relaxed visibly. 'Honey, if you want some Mexican jewellery, that ain't a problem. I'll get you some next time I'm down there.'

The road had finally bottomed out and Santa Monica lay ahead. As Burt looked over his shoulder, Cate dropped her rucksack casually on to the centre tray.

'Burt,' she shouted above the noise of his engines, 'could you stop at an ATM? I need some cash.'

He nodded and pulled over as Cate grabbed her rucksack and the phone that had been concealed underneath it. She stood with her back to the road, pretending to have a problem with the buttons on the cash machine, praying that Burt wouldn't get out of the car and come over to see what was causing the delay. As she waited for the cash to come, she slid open the back of his phone and removed the battery, then dropped in the flat card chipped with a bug that would record every single conversation Burt had on his phone. She replaced the battery and cover and pushed the phone up the sleeve of her denim jacket. She looked over her shoulder to where Burt was sitting in the car, engine still running, his fingers tapping impatiently through the open window.

Back in the car, she gave him an apologetic grin. 'Sorry to keep you waiting. Wasn't used to the instructions.'

He grunted and nodded. Then, as he went to release the handbrake, Cate felt his phone vibrate in her sleeve and emit a loud bleep. Automatically, Burt reached down between the seats. As he realised his phone wasn't there, a puzzled look spread over his handsome face.

'That yours?' said Cate, trying to sound as casual as possible, although her heart was racing. She reached on to the floor. 'Sounds as if it's coming from here.' She straightened up and handed him his phone.

'Thanks,' grunted Burt, looking down at the incoming text. Suddenly his face paled and he almost threw the phone back into the tray as if it had suddenly become red-hot.

'Where d'ya want dropping?' he said roughly, pulling back out into the traffic. 'I've got things to do.'

* * *

Santa Monica Pier was packed. Groups of tourists rubbed shoulders with young families enjoying a stroll and couples who were holding hands and taking each other's pictures. Cate passed signs for boat rides, cafés and fishing rods for hire and then, before she even reached it, she could smell and hear the funfair – the sickly aroma of candy floss, the dirty fumes from the diesel engines hazy in the sunlight, the excited screams coming from the rollercoaster which loomed high above her.

As Marcus's text had instructed, she walked over to the ticket booth, which was underneath the Big Wheel. She stood there, scanning the crowd, trying to ignore the blaring music, and waited.

Above her, the huge wheel cranked and ground its way across the bright blue sky, tiny gondolas full of people hanging from it, quivering like baubles on a Christmas tree.

She looked at her watch. Marcus was late. The music faded away and the clanking above her stopped and, as the gondolas disgorged their passengers, the next people in the queue surged forward to take their place.

'I think it's our turn.' A familiar voice spoke quietly in her ear and at the same time she felt a nudge in her back, propelling her towards an empty gondola. She didn't have to look round.

The interior of the gondola stank of stale chips and coffee, and the floor was dirty, as if it hadn't been cleaned for months. As it weaved and rocked upwards, Marcus gazed out of the window. 'I love these things,' he said. 'Always have done. Henri sends his regards, but excuses himself on the grounds that he hates heights! It's the one flaw in his otherwise robot-like brain. How are you getting on with Burt Tyler? Anything to report?'

'Give me a chance,' Cate protested. 'I only met him a few hours ago. Actually you'll be pleased to hear that I've just fitted a bug in his car, down the back of the driver's seat, and one in his phone.'

'Great work, Cate,' Marcus said enthusiastically. 'I'll get the boffins to activate the bugs. Anything else? What's your impression of him?'

'Edgy,' Cate said thoughtfully. 'Nervous. Jumps at the slightest thing. Odd really, because Mum usually goes for really laid-back types. They have to be, to cope with her.'

Cate paused, thinking hard. 'I don't know if I was imagining it, but at one point he got a text and I could have sworn Burt looked really scared when he saw the number. Yeah, scared stiff.'

Marcus was looking out of the window. He nodded thoughtfully, then turned to her, his expression grave. Suddenly Cate felt nervous.

'You haven't brought me here just to ask about Burt, have you?' Cate said. 'After all, I could have told you that on the phone.'

'You're right, Cate,' Marcus said grimly, his face suddenly stern. 'I wanted somewhere we could be safe, where I knew it was impossible to be overheard. I have to tell you some bad news. In the early hours of this morning, Gabriel Montanez was found dead in a back alley a few hundred metres from the Erin Hotel.'

Cate shook her head, trying to take it in. 'Montanez? The guy who nearly killed Ritchie and me the other night? What happened?'

'We're not sure yet,' said Marcus, 'but it looks as if he was felled by a heavy punch, hit his head on a paving slab, and died from the injuries almost instantly. In his rucksack we found a stash of dollars, an airline ticket to Spain, a false passport, a Beretta and a silencer.'

'An assassin's kit,' said Cate, half to herself. 'Was he carrying anything else?'

Marcus sighed, his dark eyes boring into hers. 'A business card belonging to Burt Tyler. And a photograph of you, with your room number at the hotel scribbled on the back. Cate, you have to know. We believe you were his target.'

CHAPTER 13

Cate took a swig of water from her bottle, swilling it around her mouth as she tried hard to quell the panic that was threatening to shut her throat and stop her breathing.

'What's going on?' she asked eventually. 'Why would anyone want to kill me? I barely know anyone in LA. I've only been here three days.'

Their gondola was at the highest possible point on the wheel now, rocking gently in the light breeze. Far below her, Cate could see people like pieces of the Playmobil that her brother used to enjoy before he got into computers. How could she be thinking about that now? she wondered vaguely.

'You're clearly a danger to them, whoever they are,' said Marcus. He shook his head. 'We have to consider the possibility that somehow someone has found out about your work with us. When you turned up here, they panicked, assumed the worst and thought you'd been sent in as an undercover agent.'

Cate stared at him, almost transfixed in horror. 'But how could that happen?' she said. 'IMIA is one of the most secure organisations in the world. Henri himself told me that. He said that only you, Marcus, and a handful of other people even knew I had worked for IMIA. It's impossible, surely, that anyone could know about that connection.'

But even as she spoke, even as she protested against it, she knew that the theory made sense. She had tried to tell herself that it was a random attack, but deep down she knew that someone had deliberately tried to run her off the road the other night.

'Ritchie said that the twins had told him something about me.' She was talking almost to herself. 'About how I was good in a crisis and had saved them from a shark attack last Christmas. But he never mentioned anything about me being a spy – and I'm sure the twins didn't know. They'd left the turtle sanctuary before the real action kicked off anyway.'

'We'll check Ritchie out, just in case,' Marcus said. 'Anyone else?'

Cate shook her head. 'Not that I can think of.'

'I'm sorry to say this, Cate,' Marcus said quietly, 'but have you considered —?'

'No,' said Cate sharply. 'Not my mother. She doesn't know anything about my work with you. I never told her – and of course Dad wouldn't either.'

'It's OK,' said Marcus, holding up his hands. 'No one's accusing her of anything. It's just that she may have inadvertently passed information on to Burt. And it's looking more and more likely that Burt is up to his neck in this whole thing.'

There was an awkward silence. Then Marcus continued in a placatory tone. 'We checked out your boat, the *Ming Yue*. It belongs to a Chinese billionaire called Xu Yongmin, head of a Shanghai steel corporation. He's had it moored here for the last year or so, pretty much for the exclusive use of his wife and daughter. Apparently, the teenage daughter is desperate to be a Hollywood actress – wants to be the next Lucy Liu. Every so often they throw huge yacht parties and invite film producers, actors, that sort of thing, hoping that she'll get her big break. Anyway, it turns out neither he nor his family have been in LA for months. He says the boat is locked up, fully secured with CCTV, and only the harbour master has the key. So whoever you saw on that boat last night, it wasn't the owner.'

'What about Novak?' Cate asked. Anything on him?'

'Now there's a strange one,' said Marcus. 'We checked him out and he does work for your friend Johnny James. According to the agency that found him the job, he did indeed come with impeccable security credentials. But when we double-checked his references, it turned out there were no records of a Novak Dabrowski. No service records, no photographs, no personal files. Nothing.'

'So the references were fake?' Cate asked. 'Can't you arrest him for that?'

'It's not quite that simple,' said Marcus. 'Lots of former agents change their name when they leave the services – assume a whole new identity and start a new life. It's a form of protection for people who've been involved in very dangerous work.'

'So you think Novak is one of those people?' asked Cate, trying to understand what Marcus was saying. 'He did do work for the security forces, but his name isn't really Novak?'

'Could be,' said Marcus. 'In any case, we've got people trying to find out. But only the very top guys know who these people are and often they won't release the details, for very good reasons. And to be honest, we haven't got a lot to convince them we have a valid need to know. Only that he was on a boat showing photographs to a Chinese businessman who says he wasn't there.'

'They were photos of Mexican antiquities,' said Cate. 'Surely that has to mean something, given your current investigation.'

Marcus pulled a face. 'You were the only one who saw them. We've got nothing to go on. If we pick him up now, everyone will know we're on to him and any contacts he has will disappear. We have to wait it out, see what other evidence we can turn up.' He put a hand on her arm. 'In any case, we don't know where Novak Dabrowski is. Not right now. The head of housekeeping at Johnny James's place confirmed that he's supposed to be somewhere in New York, on compassionate leave and not due back till next week.'

There was a loud clanking sound as the wheel began its downward journey and, despite herself, Cate jumped in her seat.

'Listen,' Marcus began. He put his hand in his pocket and pulled out an airline ticket and handed it to her. 'This is one first-class ticket back to London. We appreciate what you have done so far. You've been amazing, as usual. But we think your cover has been blown, Cate, which means you are now in real danger. You need to get out of LA. Today.'

'And then what?' Cate asked angrily. 'You arrest Burt and my mum gets dragged into something she probably has nothing to do with? I know what you guys are like. Normal rules don't apply. My mum wouldn't stand a chance.'

'That's not fair.' Marcus rubbed his eyes. 'Henri gave you his word that we would try to keep your mother out of this. But if Burt is in deep with a gang like this, then yes, she could be in serious trouble.'

'I've got a better idea,' said Cate suddenly. 'A much better idea than me running back to the UK. We – that is Mum and I – have been invited to go to Mexico tomorrow morning, with Nancy

Kyle and Lucas Black on his private jet. Lucas is filming some more footage for the fundraiser and Nancy wants us to keep her company. It's the perfect solution. It would get Mum and me safely away from LA and leave you lot to work out just who is pulling the strings behind these thugs.'

'I don't know,' Marcus said slowly. 'What if your mother tells Burt where you're staying? If he is linked to these people, you could still be at risk.

'Well, that's just it,' said Cate triumphantly. 'I wasn't actually planning on staying with them for long anyway. They don't know it yet, but I was going to leave Mum and Nancy to their swimming pools and spas and go to El Tajin – check it out and see for myself where the twins went missing. I'm going to book into one of those backpacker hostels and pass myself off as a student of Mexican history. It's the perfect cover. But I can't do it alone. I need some back-up – and an escape route. I need IMIA to promise to get me out of there if anything goes wrong. What do you say, Marcus? Are we back in business?'

Marcus gazed out of the window of the gondola. He was suddenly quiet, too quiet and Cate felt her heart lurch.

'What is it, Marcus?' she said. 'What is it you aren't telling me?'

Marcus turned to her and smiled a weak smile.

'Jeez, Cate,' he said. 'I thought I was the one who was supposed to be the experienced spy. I'd better get back to spy college.'

Cate waited patiently. Marcus was, as usual, trying to joke his way out of trouble. He shrugged and spread his long fingers wide in a gesture of surrender.

'I wasn't going to tell you. We knew that if we did we would never get you on that plane. But it looks like that's not going to happen anyway.'

Cate nodded in agreement.

'OK,' Marcus continued. 'You know we thought that there were no fatalities at the El Tajin heist?'

She nodded again, this time trying to quell the nauseous fear that was rising from her stomach.

'They found two bodies in the jungle a few kilometres inland from the camp. The government knew about it but chose, for their own reasons, not to tell us right away.

'Not the twins – don't worry.' Marcus laid a reassuring hand on Cate's suddenly clammy arm. 'It was the guards from the camp.' Marcus's face tightened in anger. 'Hands tied behind their backs and shot through the head. Young men, family men, both of them. Just doing their job.'

Cate looked at him in horror. She felt a stab of guilt that, for a few seconds, she had been relieved that it was the guards and not her friends. But at least now she knew the real truth about just how ruthless this gang could be.

'I have to go,' Cate said suddenly. 'I have to get down there to at least try to find the twins. You know, Marcus, I could be just the one to do it.'

The wheel had nearly completed its circuit now. A few more minutes and they would be out in the world again, and she would be facing – what? A bullet through her head? Bundled into a van and taken somewhere quiet to be disposed of. Cate shuddered. Marcus was right about one thing: she had to get out of this town fast. But he was talking again, more to himself, Cate thought, than to her.

'It's one thing sending you in to spy for us when people think you're just a regular sixteen-year-old kid. But we can't just ignore the fact that someone almost certainly knows who you are. If something happens to you, not only will I feel personally responsible, but your father will probably hunt us down like the mad dogs we are. And I can't say I'll blame him either.'

'OK, Marcus, how about a compromise?' Cate put on her reasonable voice. 'Let's ask Henri and whatever he says, we'll go with it. Deal?'

The wheel juddered to a halt and the door was pulled open by a bored-looking youth.

'Deal,' said Marcus reluctantly as he stepped down from the gondola and scanned the crowd with eagle eyes. As she alighted behind him, Cate noticed for the first time a bulge underneath his jacket, just above his waistline. As usual, Marcus had come ready for trouble.

'I must say, I like the idea of having an undercover agent checking out El Tajin.' Henri, his voice hammering like a machine gun out of the speaker on Marcus's phone, had been as pragmatic as always, just as Cate suspected he would. 'We were talking about putting someone in there anyway and Cate speaks pretty good Spanish, as I recall. It's amazing what you can pick up if you listen. The locals often hang out with the backpackers, people have a few beers, tongues get loose. It's a good idea. But with a potential price on Cate's head, well, I don't know if we can take that risk. We may have to end up bailing her out of trouble and we really can't afford the manpower at the moment. As far as IMIA is concerned, Cate may well be a spent force.'

Cate took a sharp intake of breath and Marcus shot her an apologetic glance. Tact was never Henri's strongest point.

Oblivious, Henri tutted to himself, clearly thinking hard. 'I have to consider this. I'll let you know as soon as I reach a decision. In the meantime, Marcus, take Cate somewhere secure. She's no longer safe in LA.

Five minutes later, Cate found herself looking up at the dirty windows of an apartment over a cut-price grocery store three blocks back from the ocean.

'We're not in a James Bond movie,' said Marcus as he spotted the disappointment on her face. 'Real spies blend into the background; they don't drive flash cars and live in penthouse suites. We're not even good-looking. Well, present company excepted, of course. In fact, a good spy is delighted if no one can ever remember what he or she looks like. Stay there.' He gestured towards the porch. 'I'll just check we weren't followed.'

Once inside the grubby two-roomed apartment, Cate sat down gingerly on a rather dirty cream sofa.

'Fancy a cup of tea?' Marcus waved a couple of chipped mugs at her. 'Though there's no milk, I'm afraid.'

Cate shook her head.

'Game of cards?' Marcus produced a pack from his pocket and began to deal. 'Pontoon?'

Cate had just beaten Marcus for the third time in a row when his phone bleeped softly.

'Henri says to go ahead,' he said, looking up from his phone. 'Oh, and apparently Novak Dabrowski left the Polish security services three years ago. Which begs the question, where has he been in the meantime?'

A few minutes later there was a gentle knock at the door.

'Yo, Jay,' said Marcus, high-fiving with the bespectacled young black man carrying a large, battered briefcase. 'Haven't seen you since that Croatian deal went down. Was it three years ago? Oh, by the way, this is Cate, your operative. I guess you've been told what she needs.'

Jay looked at Cate, opened his mouth and then shut it again. He put his bag down and began to unpack the contents on to the glass coffee table.

Cate spotted the standard spy stuff: a few bugs, a compact bundle of dollar notes, a microscopic infra-red camera hidden in a pen, a tiny laser that could cut through just about anything. Funny, she reflected, how she knew exactly what they were. When she had first used these gadgets last summer she had thought that they were amazing, so complicated that she would never be able to use them. But now, after two missions, they felt almost like old friends – familiar, easy-to-use and totally reliable. Perhaps this spying thing was growing on her after all.

'What's this?' she asked, picking up what looked like a conductor's baton and waving it around.

'Aha – clever little thing, this is,' said Jay, putting out his hand. His breath smelled of chewing gum and coffee. 'It's new, but very sensitive and reliable. It's a metal detector, see?'

He pulled a tiny attachment from the bottom of the small leather bag and pushed it on to the tip of the rod. He waved it over Cate's hand and it bleeped happily at the silver Tiffany ring that Monique and her dad had given her for her sixteenth birthday present.

'It's accurate to a distance of about three metres. Flick this switch here . . .' he pointed to a tiny red knob at the side of the baton '. . . and it becomes a heat-seeker.'

'Useful for searching out live targets,' explained Marcus, seeing her puzzled face. 'Even works through solid stone. We thought it might come in handy, as you're going to be hanging out in the pyramids!'

'Ever worn contact lenses?' Jay asked her.

Cate shook her head, taken aback at the question. She had twenty-twenty vision, unlike Arthur and her friend Louisa.

'I'd like you to practise wearing these.'

Cate took the small plastic tin from him and, to her

amazement, opened it up to find a pair of clear eye lenses cupped in a bed of blue fluid.

'You want me to wear contact lenses?' She was baffled.

'At Christmas we kitted you out with night-vision goggles,' Marcus reminded her. 'This is the next step up. Night-vision lenses. Safe, secure, easy to use. State of the art, ultra high-tech, they mould to the shape of your eye and give you the clearest daytime vision in the darkest of places.'

'Wow,' Cate said. 'That really is incredible. Who on earth thought of that?'

'The military,' said Jay, his eyes dancing enthusiastically behind his thick glasses. 'Like with most of these inventions. It's usually them or the gaming industry. We've been using these since January and, I can tell you, it's a lifesaving bit of kit. And you never know – you might just need it.'

Suddenly Marcus had an uncharacteristically worried expression on his face. 'Cate, I promise you we'll stay in close touch and if you come across anything in your investigations in Mexico, anything at all that you think warrants back-up, call us and we'll get to you as quickly as we can. Just use my safe number or Skype us at HQ. And promise me you won't take any unnecessary risks.'

Cate looked at him and then over to Jay. She picked up the gadgets and almost lovingly loaded them into her rucksack. 'You can rely on me,' she said.

CHAPTER 14

The turquoise swimming pool shimmered and glittered in the warm sunshine. Somewhere nearby, a waterfall was tinkling gently into a miniature lake teeming with exotic fish. Cate lay on a sun lounger, enthralled by the sounds of the forest, the deep throb of the hummingbirds and the shrieks of the parakeets coming from the lush tropical greenery that surrounded the hotel grounds, grateful for the distraction they provided to her endlessly churning thoughts.

Behind her lay the vast marble edifice of the smartest hotel in Veracruz, a place that, with its vast oil paintings and gleaming stone floors, reminded Cate more of a cathedral than somewhere to rest her head. It was situated almost directly on the main plaza, a huge cobblestone square edged by vast, gracious colonial buildings built on arches, underneath which a bewildering array of vendors and musicians plied their trade to tourists and locals alike.

The limousine had dropped them off just by the square and, as the numerous cases – most of them leather, very heavy and belonging to Nancy – were being unloaded by a flurry of overexcited hotel porters, Cate wandered a few metres away. Her phone beeped. It was a text from Ritchie. Cate had a sudden pang of guilt. She had forgotten to tell him she was going to Mexico. But now, knowing what she knew, she was loathe to tell anyone where she was.

A group of Spanish guitar players had struck up a fast and furious melody that quickly had people around them clapping and stamping in time to the music. Several stalls were enjoying a roaring trade in lunchtime food; the aromas of paprika, shellfish and coffee wafted towards the new arrivals.

'I love this city.' Lucas was suddenly at her side. 'I always use it as my base when I come to Mexico, even though it's a few hours from where I'll be doing the filming. It's so full of history and atmosphere. They call Veracruz the crossroads of the Americas – and with good reason. Wars, invasions, pirates and traders from every corner of the globe – all human life either has been or is here.'

He paused and then his voice hardened. 'What are you up to, Cate? The other night at the restaurant I went to the loo shortly after you did. And guess what? I saw you following someone and clambering on to a boat. Peering through a window. Spying.' His voice turned angry almost. 'I'm guessing that you have somehow decided that it would be sensible to work with IMIA again when we both know how dangerous they are.'

Cate stared at him, her guilt rendering her dumb, her usually quick-witted mind frozen. She knew she could trust Lucas, and that thanks to his army days in counter-intelligence he understood how organisations like IMIA worked. But how much could she tell him? How far could she push his loyalty?

She took a deep breath. 'Some friends of mine have gone missing from El Tajin, where they were working on an archaeological dig. When IMIA found out I was in LA, they contacted me and asked me if I could get down there and start asking some questions. They thought that a teenager working undercover might give them an advantage.'

Lucas was silent for minute. 'Are you in danger?'

'I don't think so. Well, not now I'm down here – and as long as no one knows where I've gone when I go to El Tajin. So please, don't tell anyone, Lucas. And I mean no one.'

He stared at her, visibly shocked. 'Not even your mother?'

Cate felt her face burning at the realisation that she was admitting, not just to herself but also to Lucas, that she couldn't trust her own mother. 'I can't risk her stopping me,' she lied, feeling more miserable by the second. 'But if I don't go and at least try to help find my friends, well, I'll never forgive myself.'

Lucas's face finally softened. 'You're obsessed with saving the world. Or trying to. God knows why. It's not as if you actually make a difference. Not really.'

'You are too,' Cate said. 'Look why you're here in Mexico.'

'Sometimes I think I'd be better off just buying a vineyard. Making cheese. Going on reality TV shows,' Lucas replied. He sighed. 'I'm not going to stop you, Cate. I can't. But I'm telling you one thing: you may be clever, you may be brave, but you've also been damn lucky so far. The army taught us that you can never rely on luck because, sure as hell, one day it will run out.'

Her phone bleeped. It was another text from Ritchie.

Where r u? Hv I offended u? Can we meet 4 coffee? Need 2 talk.

Cate felt a pang of guilt. Poor Ritchie. She had just cleared off without telling him anything. And after all they had been through that terrible night together too. No wonder he wanted to meet.

She frowned. It felt mean not to reply to him. Surely it

wouldn't do any harm to let him know she was out of town, so long as she kept the details vague.

Gone away with Lucas, Nancy and Mum for a break. Call u when back in LA.

Now, sitting by the hotel pool, Cate reached under her sunbed and pulled out her tablet, then looked around her carefully. There was no one nearby, even the waiters had vanished back into the cool of the hotel. She looked at her watch. Two p.m. Evening in London.

Arthur had a bowl of cereal in his hand.

'Arthur,' Cate began. 'I've made it to Mexico. I'm here with Mum too – but not for long. I'm planning to break away – get up to El Tajin. Just to check it out. But I can't tell Mum, not till I've gone.'

'I wish you luck,' said Arthur. 'She'll be pretty mad. She sent me an email saying she'd hardly seen you since you arrived in LA. Seems to think you've got yourself a new boyfriend.'

Cate blushed. 'No way!' she cried. 'Ritchie is a lovely guy but, well, he's just a friend. And, you know, I've only recently split up with Michel. Anyway, did you find anything out?' Cate continued, quickly changing the subject.

'Weeeelll.' Arthur was clearly enjoying himself. 'You know you gave me the names of all those sites that had been attacked? You wanted me to try and find out any links between them that marked them out as a target?'

Cate nodded.

'I tried all sorts of things. Where they were sited, how old they were, the cultures that built them, the type of stuff they were excavating, how big or small. I even tried their geographical coordinates.'

'And?' prompted Cate. 'Any luck?'

'Nothing.' Arthur sat back in his chair. 'Not a thing. Apart from the fact they were all digs in Mexico and by the coast – which we knew already – I couldn't find one thing to link them.'

Cate tried hard to hide her disappointment. Another possible lead gone.

'At least you tried, Arthur,' she said kindly. 'You can't win 'em all.'

'Ahem.' There was a small cough from the screen. 'Actually, I think I can claim yet another victory for the geek in your life! I decided to take a step back. An overview, as they say. Perhaps it wasn't the sites themselves that were providing the common thread, perhaps it was the victims. It appears that, as in Europe, archaeological digs in Mexico are pretty tightly regulated. You can't just turn up and start excavating ancient sites. You have to be properly organised, even if you are just a small team, overseen by the Department of Archaeology at the University of Mexico City.'

'Right,' said Cate. She wasn't quite sure where this was going but Arthur was clearly on a roll.

'I was up most of last night, but finally I managed to find a way into their departmental system. Then it took a few likely keywords and up it popped. A spreadsheet containing all the archaeological sites in Mexico, who's currently working on them, which university they're from and so on. I saw El Tajin, of course, with the four names including your friends Amber and Jade. I ran the spreadsheet against the names of the five sites which had been attacked and there was a link . . .'

Cate sat forward on the bed, her heart racing. 'Go on, Arthur, tell me. I can't bear the suspense.'

'It was the money,' Arthur said triumphantly. 'Archaeological digs don't come cheap and to keep going they all need outside sponsorships. Some of the sites are openly sponsored by big corporations. BD Oil, for example. Cervaza beer is another one. In return, they get to display their logos – in the site museum, say – trumpet their goodness in the media, bring their employees up for festivals and so on.'

'Seems fair enough,' said Cate. 'They're going to expect something in return.'

'Agreed. But our digs were all funded by the same company in what looked like a highly confidential and secretive agreement, asking for nothing in return. In fact, there's a warning note on the spreadsheet that the company has specifically stipulated no publicity. Wanna know the name of the company?'

'Oh Arthur, you're such a tease.' Cate grinned at her brother. 'Of course I do.'

'Johnny James Holdings. Head office in LA, bank accounts filed in the Caymen Islands. For tax reasons probably.'

Cate stared at her brother. 'Johnny James.' Somewhere a light was going on in her brain. What had Ritchie said about his uncle?

Johnny James had agreed to sponsor the twins, paid for everything. If he hadn't, they wouldn't have been able to go.

'JJ Holdings is the umbrella company for a variety of smaller enterprises,' continued Arthur. 'Including a film production company, a record label, and, of course, the hotel where you were staying – the Erin Hotel in Santa Monica.'

'So Johnny James wasn't just sponsoring the twins. He was funding digs all over Mexico,' Cate said slowly. 'And for some reason he doesn't want anyone to know about it and doesn't seem to want anything in return. Why, when he is such a publicity seeker in other areas for his charitable work?'

Arthur shrugged. 'Dunno, sis. I leave the clever stuff to you.'

'Arthur,' said Cate suddenly. Her heart was racing now. For the first time in this seemingly unsolvable mystery it seemed they could just be one step ahead of the criminals. 'Are there others on the list – other digs that JJ Holdings are sponsoring that haven't been attacked yet? If we can find that out – well, we might be able to prevent the next heist, or use it to catch whoever's responsible.'

'Yeah, of course, sorry. I've got them here. I'll text them to you.'

'Wicked, Arthur,' said Cate admiringly. 'Top of the class today. I'll pass them on to Marcus right away. And now, just in case you get bored, I've got another little job for you. I need you to check out a yacht, a boat called *Ming Yue* – which I think means *Bright Moon*. Owned by a Chinese billionaire called Xu Yongmin.'

'What am I looking for?'

'I dunno,' said Cate thoughtfully. 'Anything that could link the boat to the twins, to Mexico, I guess. I want to know why Novak Dabrowski was showing photographs of Mexican antiquities to a man onboard the boat when he was supposed to be in New York and the boat was meant to be locked up.'

Arthur shrugged. 'I'll see what I can do. I haven't done much work in China. It'll be an education. Do you mind if I finish my supper now? It's not often I can convince Monique to buy Coco Pops, but she felt sorry for me because you're away and gave in to pester power. A bit like I always give in to your pester power!' He grinned and blew Cate a kiss. 'And before you ask, no, I won't save any for you. They're mine, all mine!'

CHAPTER 15

The ancient bus clanked and groaned its way along the coastal highway, jumping violently over enormous speed bumps, the smoking engine protesting loudly at every rise and turn in the road. On one side, the Gulf of Mexico shimmered out to the horizon, the early-morning blue broken only by a never-ending stream of supertankers heading south to Cape Horn and on to the South Atlantic.

The vivid greens of citrus groves groaned with half-grown oranges; lemons and grapefruits stretched away into the distance. Beyond them lay the beautiful yet forbidding peaks of the volcanic mountain range, fringed with the lush colours of the rainforest.

Cate stared out of the chipped and pockmarked window and tried hard to suppress feelings of excitement and fear. Somewhere, up in those hills, pretty much in the middle of a jungle, lay El Tajin.

Cate had done her homework. El Tajin was built by the Totonacs nearly thirteen hundred years ago. At the height of its power, between around 1000 and 1200 AD, the city was home to twenty-five thousand people who mingled and lived amongst spectacular pyramids, temples and streets with an influence that extended hundreds of kilometres along the coastline.

The city even had seventeen ball courts for a game played by ancient Mexican tribes such as the Huastecs. Even saying the names sounded exotic and mysterious, thought Cate.

But there was another darker side to El Tajin. The name meant 'the place of the invisible beings or spirits' and, according to one website Cate had found, the Spanish conquistadores who came across the deserted ruins when they invaded Mexico had another name for El Tajin. They called it Mictlan, the abode of the dead.

Despite the warmth of the sun beaming through the windows, Cate felt a shiver running down her spine. To distract herself, she pulled out her tablet and opened a file she had filled with information about the site.

According to Wikipedia, the city was finally looted, then destroyed by fire by an invading force called the Chichimecs. The residents fled and founded a town nearby called Papantla, leaving their city to the mercy of the voracious jungle which quickly consumed it. And there it lay silent and untouched, for the next five hundred years, until discovered by accident – and today it was a world heritage site.

Cate brought herself reluctantly back to the present. It was ten past nine. Her mother would be waking up about now, reading the note that Cate had left on her pillow just as she crept out of the suite they were sharing.

Mum. Didn't want to wake you. Had a text from friends who are camping in the jungle for a couple of days. I've gone to meet them, but will be back for the return flight. Have fun! I'll text you when I get there. Cate xx

Cate knew she should really have told her mother that she was going to El Tajin, but she had been terrified that she would have stopped her, insisting that she stayed in Veracruz. And she didn't want her mother inadvertently passing on her whereabouts to Burt. All in all, a note had seemed the only safe option.

As the bus began to haul itself up a long, winding hill, she looked around at her fellow passengers with interest. Although the bus had left the main square of Veracruz at a ridiculously early hour, it was still packed – mainly with local people. Sitting at the back, a dark-haired man reading a guidebook reminded her uncomfortably of Burt. She sighed, put her tablet back into her rucksack, and leaned her forehead against the grubby window and tried to think.

Burt. He had to know Gabriel, his card was found in the dead man's rucksack. But Novak – how did he fit in?

She closed her eyes, thinking back to that terrible night when she and Ritchie had very nearly lost their lives. Gabriel had been driving the truck – Burt's truck. Stolen, Burt had said, from Mexicano Magic.

She forced herself to concentrate. The man who had pushed her into the bomb shelter at her mother's shop; she hadn't seen his face, not once, but she had heard his voice, hissing in her ear. *'Drop the phone, kid, or you're dead. Drop it.'*

She sat bolt upright. Her mind scrolled forward, to another horror: a man shouting at her, running after the truck in the pull-in on the Pacific Highway as she took photographs of him from her iPhone. *'Drop the phone, kid, or you're dead. Drop it.'*

The same words. The same angry voice. The driver of the truck that nearly killed her and Ritchie, and the ruthless thug at Mexicano Magic. They were the same person. Gabriel Montanez. She was sure of it.

Cate stared unseeing out of the window, her mind going back to the scene at Mexicano Magic. The two Mexicans had been adamant they weren't doing anything wrong, that they were just doing their job. They had been so convincing that she had believed them.

Her mind flashed to the crates she had seen stacked against the wall at the back of the shop, stamped with Spanish instructions. She had assumed the crates were for Burt's business, but perhaps they hadn't been carrying cheap Mexican tat after all. Perhaps the crates had been holding treasure. Ancient treasure looted at gunpoint from sites all over Mexico. No wonder they had panicked when they saw her, no wonder Gabriel was furious at the thought she may have seen what was inside those crates.

Her heart was racing. She was sure she must be right. Mexicano Magic was the drop-off point for the stolen treasure, brought in by Gabriel and then distributed to buyers.

But who was behind it all? Surely not a hired thug like Gabriel. This operation was highly sophisticated, requiring a huge amount of money and planning, not to mention contacts on both side of the border. She shook her head. She still had a lot of thinking to do.

Was she right to be heading for El Tajin? Did the answer to the mystery lie, after all, in LA, at Mexicano Magic? How did Burt fit in?

She decided she would have to leave Burt to Marcus and Henri. The most important thing was to find the twins and work out why they went missing from El Tajin. And she sensed she didn't have much time. After all it was already four days since she had heard that the twins were missing, nearly a week since they were taken. Wherever they were, the odds of finding them alive must surely be lessening with each passing hour.

Despite her gnawing anxiety, she must have dozed off, for suddenly the bus was juddering down through the gears. Cate opened her eyes blearily and saw they were on a narrow street crowded with stalls and vendors selling everything from rugs, clothes and stone statues to food and drink. The bus weaved through the stalls, tooting impatiently at anyone who strayed into its path.

The bus finally pulled to a halt and the doors opened with a huge, steaming hiss. Cate grabbed her rucksack and stepped eagerly out. They had arrived at El Tajin!

Her first reaction was one of disappointment. The dusty concrete road was scruffy and cracked, edged with parched-looking plants. Above her, a tatty Mexican flag fluttered forlornly in the thin breeze. As she looked towards the entrance of the ruins, rather than pyramids and vast stone statues, all she could see were two tubby round concrete blocks, with all the appeal of a power station.

She followed the trickle of people walking towards the entrance. She had a stack of things to do, but she couldn't resist at least a quick look at the ruins first. Afterwards, she would get to work, find a hostel and check in, Skype Arthur and update Marcus.

Cate reached the entrance to the site and found herself passing through a small turnstile into a courtyard surrounded on three sides by low concrete buildings which contained the museum, a visitors' centre and a shop. She joined the queue which led towards the ticket office and paid in cash for a pass that allowed her a week's unrestricted access to the site.

Her excitement growing, she followed the signs which were written in both Spanish and English and headed down a narrow, grassy path, a hedge of trees blocking out any view of what lay to either side.

Then the hedge disappeared, the path widened out, and suddenly Cate was standing still, awestruck at her first sight of El Tajin.

She had seen countless images, but nothing could have prepared her for the sheer spectacle of what lay before her. Cate was standing in the centre of a square. In front of her, to the left and to the right, were huge pyramids, perfect 3D triangles, rising up, step by step, block by block, and topped by grass rectangles.

She looked down at her guidebook. This was the religious centre of the city, the place where ancient ceremonies of worship and sacrifice had been made – and even now, one thousand years on, Cate could see how utterly incredible and awesome a sight they must have been.

She walked slowly around and through the crumbling pyramids, marvelling, absorbing, observing. She spotted the rectangular ball courts, the walls around them beautifully decorated with artistic depictions of the game that once was played there, and she ran her fingers over the carved stone pillars found at the entrance to many of the buildings.

Presiding over it all, looming at the top of a sharply rising grassy slope, stood the vast Pyramid of the Niches. It was a huge edifice of stone stairs rising ever upwards, each layer of pyramid marked out by myriad small, square windows sunk into the stonework, three hundred and sixty-five in all – one for each day of the year.

Cate walked towards it and stared up, half fascinated, half fearful of its splendour. Her gaze was drawn to the niches, dark unseeing eyes, keeping watch over the ancient place of worship.

The jungle seemed to encroach on the site and she could hear the sinister shrieking of birds, the harsh barking of monkeys and despite the bright sunshine she felt uneasy, jittery even. For a few seconds she desperately wanted to return to the safety of Veracruz and the easy company of Nancy and her mother, but then she got a grip, laughing at herself. She was letting the majesty and history of the site get to her. They were just old buildings. She had a job to do and she was going to get on with it.

Cate dragged herself reluctantly away from the pyramids and headed back down towards the entrance. She would leave the exploration of the rest of the site to another time. Now she had to sort out a place to stay.

'There's a couple of backpacker hostels on the far side of the site,' Marcus had explained. 'They're mainly for students or people studying the ruins who want to stay close to them rather than go back and forth to the town everyday. They're full of people coming and going, all ages, all nationalities. It's the perfect place to go undercover. Nose around the site, take a look at where the students were staying. Talk to people who might have been staying at the hostels for a while. Someone must know something. Pass on any information to us as quickly as possible.' He looked at her sternly. 'We don't want anything else from you. So, leave the heroics to us. Got it?'

The long two-storey timber building sat neatly at the edge of the jungle, surrounded on three sides by lush greenery. The front faced out towards El Tajin, which stood a good two hundred metres away. The blue shutters were tightly closed against the midday sun and an air of sleepy stillness surrounded the hostel. Only the sound of cicadas humming in the long grasses and the quiet rushing sound of nearby water disturbed the silence.

Cate spotted a double door over which a small sign proclaimed itself to be the reception. She headed through and found herself inside a large hall. The entire building, inside and out, had clearly been constructed using local timber – the tell-tale dark wood of the mahogany tree was evident in the floorboards, the wooden panelling, and even on the stairway that led up to the first floor.

It was cooler inside than out, but not much. Above her, large fans hummed and whirred.

'*Hola, senorita*,' a friendly voice called to her. 'Can I help you, Miss?'

Sitting on a tall stool at the end of the bar was a woman in her twenties.

'*Muchas gracias*,' Cate said in reply. 'I'm looking for a place to stay. Do you have any rooms?'

'You American? English?' The woman slid down from her barstool.

'*Si*,' Cate said. '*Ingles*. Is my accent that bad?'

The woman smiled. 'No, no, it's very good. But working here, you get to know. So how long are you planning on staying?'

Cate put her rucksack down on the wooden floor and pretended to consider. 'Maybe few days, maybe a week,' she said. 'What have you got?'

'If you pay for a week you can have a room to yourself,' said the woman, picking up a clipboard and scrutinising it. 'It's more expensive, but it has a lock on the door and a private loo. You share the showers. Otherwise, if you're staying for a couple of days you'll have to go in a dorm. They're OK. Clean and very cheap. You just have to put up with people snoring. Oh and this is a females-only hostel. If you're after a man, you've come to the wrong place! Don't worry – the men's hostel is just a few hundred metres from here!' she said, smiling.

'I'll take the room,' Cate said. 'I'll pay now.' She reached into an inside pocket of her rucksack and pulled out her money.'

'Welcome to the Hostel Volodores,' the woman said. 'My name is Maria. Any problems, you need anything, you come to me. Now, let me take your passport details.'

She placed the clipboard down on the counter, took Cate's passport and disappeared through a small doorway into an office. Cate scanned the guest list to see if any of the names meant anything to her.

'You looking for something?' Maria was back, silently, without warning, making Cate jump guiltily. She didn't seem annoyed.

'Just checking to see if my friends are staying here,' Cate said, unable to meet her eye. 'They were travelling in this area and we thought we might meet up.'

'No problem,' said Maria good-naturedly. 'What are their names? If they've been here in the last few weeks, I'll be able to tell you.'

'Amber and Jade Harvey,' said Cate suddenly, watching Maria's face closely. 'They're twins. From California. They were working on the dig here. Did you know them?'

In the silence that followed, Cate could hear the humming of a fridge and the quiet chatter of voices drifting down the stairway.

Maria's face was drained of colour. She looked, Cate thought, as if she had seen a ghost. 'They were nice girls,' she said quietly. 'Friendly. They came here to play cards and drink coffee with the backpackers.' Cate saw real fear in Maria's eyes. 'You know what happened? I'm terribly sorry to have to tell you. The girls and their friends have vanished.'

Her face crumpled and for a minute Cate thought she was going to cry. She started to tell Cate all about it. 'It was very bad,' she said finally. 'Horrible. The guards, they were good friends of mine, they were taken too. And we heard that they are dead. Shot. The police came and told us not to scare the tourists. That we should keep quiet. I shouldn't even be talking to you now.'

'The twins, they are good friends of mine,' said Cate. 'Their mother is sick, she has no other children.'

Maria shook her head. 'Poor woman,' she said sympathetically.

Cate pressed on. 'If you know anything, noticed anything that could point to what happened, could you tell me?'

'There was something,' Maria said. 'I told the police about it. That night I was parked in a lay-by on the road from El Tajin. I was meeting my boyfriend, you understand?' Maria looked sheepish. 'It is difficult. He has a wife so he has to sneak out when she is asleep.'

Cate nodded, keeping her face expressionless even though inside she could feel the excitement bubbling up. This sounded very interesting.

'We were there from maybe eleven p.m. until first light – maybe four or fiveish. When I got back to the camp the guards and the students were gone.'

She paused and took a swig of Coke from a plastic bottle on the counter. 'So I swear that whoever it was, they didn't come in or leave by the road. Not one vehicle passed us the whole time we were in the lay-by. Not one. And if they had come in by plane or helicopter, Juan and me, we would have heard them too.' She looked Cate straight in the eye. 'Whoever did this, they must have already been at the site. And maybe they still haven't left it.'

Chapter 16

Cate closed the door of her room and locked it carefully. Then she sat down on the narrow bed which lay underneath the window and took a deep breath.

Maybe Maria had been so distracted by her boyfriend that she had missed a vehicle going past. Or perhaps they had fallen asleep for a few minutes. But she had certainly been convincing.

Cate drummed her fingers on the white sheets. Was it possible that the attackers had come out from the forest and, after the attack, escaped that way? Perhaps their vehicles had been parked miles away and they had marched their prisoners there. Or perhaps, she thought with a shudder, they had disposed of their prisoners en route.

She pulled out her tablet, switching it on and plugging it in, and waited while it searched for the hostel's wifi signal. The security measures Arthur had fitted to her tablet would make sure all her communications stayed secure. Cate firmly believed that there wasn't a hacker on this earth who could break Arthur's security codes.

There was a soft bleep as the signal reached full strength, then a harder buzzing signifying that someone was trying to reach her on Skype.

'Hey, Cate – how are things in deepest Mexico?' Arthur was excited about something. His hair stood up on his head, forced upright from running his fingers through it, which he always did when his brain was working overtime.

'Amazing,' Cate said, 'in more ways than one. The site is just incredible. But it's kinda spooky too.'

'Cool,' said Arthur. He wasn't really listening, Cate could tell.

'Come on, Arthur,' she said encouragingly. 'Out with it. What's the hot news?'

Her brother pulled a goofy face. 'Erm, just wondered if you'd heard from your Michel by any chance?'

Cate's heart turned a neat somersault in her chest at the mention of her ex-boyfriend's name.

'Michel? No, nothing. And he's not *my* Michel anyway. He's not my anything. In case you'd forgotten, he dumped me.' Curiosity got the better of her, though. 'Why do you ask?'

Arthur raised his eyebrows enigmatically. 'Well, I'm not quite sure how to break this to you but, well . . . he's just turned up. At the house. He's downstairs talking to Monique and Dad right now.'

They stared at each other for a few seconds. Then a huge grin broke out on Arthur's face, one which Cate knew was mirrored on her own.

'Excuse me, Arthur, for one minute,' she said, picking up a pillow from the bed. 'I just need to . . .'

'Have a good scream,' her brother finished for her. 'Go on, sis, get it out of your system.'

'That's better,' said Cate, thirty seconds later, as she

repositioned herself in front of the screen and pulled her ponytail back into place. 'Now I want you to tell me everything. What exactly did Michel say? How does he look? Is he still gorgeous? *Why has he come to London?*'

Cate suddenly realised that she was no longer looking at the pixellated features of her kid brother. Instead, she found herself staring into the handsome, smiling face of her ex-boyfriend.

'I came to London because I needed to see you,' said Michel, his big, brown eyes sparkling with amusement. 'I have missed you so much. I was stupid and stubborn and I refused to see things from your point of view . . .'

'Oh Michel,' said Cate. Her heart was suddenly soaring. 'I don't blame you. I would have done the same.'

Michel looked serious. 'No, you would have listened to me, given me a chance to really explain my side of the story. I didn't and I'm stupid and I'm sorry. Can you forgive me?'

Cate grinned happily. 'Of course I forgive you. I've missed you so much. How are you? How's work, your family? Oh, I so wish I was back in London. Or better still, in Antibes.'

'Me too,' said Michel. 'That is typical of us. I finally pluck up the courage to come to London and you've gone to LA. But this time, Cate, I'm not letting you get away. As soon as you get back to London – the very minute you do – I'll be here waiting for you. If I don't see you soon I think I will go – what's the word you use? – bonkers.'

'Michel, I'm counting the days. I've been going bonkers too.'

They chatted some more, but eventually they had to put an end to the conversation. Cate lay back on the pillow, a huge grin on her face. Michel had forgiven her, they were back together, he would be waiting for her in London. Just wait till she told Louisa.

Her mobile ringing jarred her back to reality. Cate looked

162

down at the screen and pulled a face. It was her mother and even the ring tone seemed angry.

Reluctantly she hit the receive button. At the sound of her mother's furious voice shrieking down the line, Cate settled back on to the bed. She had no defence, she knew that. All she could do was shut her eyes and wait for the storm to blow itself out. But did she care? Michel was back in her life. Nothing else mattered any more!

The hut where the archaeology students had stayed was situated well away from the tourist area on a patch of land hacked from the jungle and next to a fast-running river.

Cate approached the site carefully, checking continuously that no one was following her, keeping a wary eye out for the security guards she had seen wandering around the ruins earlier in the day.

Signs of the excavation work were everywhere – gaping ditches with pieces of stone protruding out of them like teeth in an open mouth, a tall stone pillar topped with the half-missing face of a warrior, and the first few steps of a pyramid, crumbling, almost unrecognisable from the fully restored beauties Cate had seen earlier on the official site.

Everywhere, the jungle was encroaching. Strangely shaped roots burst through the dry ground, thick carpets of grass and weeds reached across even the new excavations. Just then, a pair of macaws strutted out of the jungle, the bright reds and yellows of their plumage providing a vivid contrast to the dull green. Their sharp, dark eyes seemed to look at Cate fearlessly.

'Hello,' said Cate, so entranced by the sight that for a moment she forgot what she was there for. 'You're beautiful.' One of them shrieked at Cate loudly, then plucked crossly at the ground in front of her, pulling out tiny insects with easy skill.

Cate smiled and looked across at the hut. It was raised up on low timber stilts, the space between the floor and the ground outside a good half-metre. Thick grass and sinuous roots formed an almost impenetrable barrier between the two. At the back, the jungle had been allowed to grow up against the timber walls and Cate could see spiny plants and hairy vines creeping around the sides of the building.

It was clearly deserted. The only sign that the police had been there was a ripped *Do not enter – crime scene* banner strewn carelessly across the front. Cate shook her head, shocked at how insecure the hut was. She glanced over her shoulder, then pushed cautiously at the wooden door. It opened easily, revealing a low-ceilinged interior which already smelled damp and dank, as if it had lain unused for months instead of just a few days.

As Cate's eyes adjusted to the gloom, she saw two sets of bunk beds divided by a thin plywood partition. The bedding had gone, presumably taken by the police for forensic evidence, leaving only a thin sheet covering each mattress. Mosquito nets hung from hooks on the ceiling like ghostly waterfalls.

It was easy to see which had been the twins' bunks. The wall between the top and bottom bed was plastered with photographs, leaving hardly any space between them. Cate felt a sadness well up in her as she saw pictures of the twins hiking, dancing with friends, hugging someone who was presumably their mother, hanging out on the beach. There was even a group photograph of the gang from Snapper Bay, and Cate saw, with a lump in her throat, that she was in it, her arm flung carelessly around a beaming, handsome Michel.

She turned to the books stashed on a small bedside table by the bunks. The twins were obviously taking their assignment seriously – most of the books were archaeological reference books, travel books covering Mexico, and a few biographies of world-famous explorers, dozens of the pages marked with yellow sticky notes. Cate smiled then, remembering Jade's jokey profile on her Twitter page: *Aiming to be the most famous explorer since Colombus.*

She walked around the partition and peered through the gloom at the other beds. On the bottom bunk, action shots of football jostled with photographs of female popstars and actresses and posters for heavy metal gigs. Funny how you could tell so much so quickly about people, just by looking at a few of their possessions, mused Cate.

Her phone twitched into life. Phone reception here? She was surprised, and imagined it was sporadic at best.

Hey Cate. Need 2 talk. Where are u? Call me? Ritchie.

Dammit. Michel's call had completely blown Ritchie out of her mind. She made a mental note to text him again later.

Cate looked around curiously. On one side there was a large wooden desk and a bookshelf filled mainly with maps and charts. Above the desk hung a map of the area surrounding the hut, marking the latest excavation sites. She perched on the edge of the desk and gazed out of the small window. The group had found something here, something important enough to warrant the leader of the dig calling in one of the most important professors in Mexico. And Cate was sure that, if she worked out what that was, she would be much closer to finding out just what had happened to the twins.

She began to search along the shelves, sifting methodically through the books and folded maps, looking for signs of any recent use. Some of the charts dated back as far as the nineteen-twenties, the time when the restoration of the site had begun, and most of them were covered in dust and clearly hadn't been unfolded for some time. The books were a disappointment, nothing more than a random collection of cheap paperbacks and ancient hardbacks, probably what passed for entertainment when the day's work was done.

She moved on to the desk drawers. The discovery of a logbook gave Cate a quick moment of hope, but even that proved to be a disappointment. Apart from mundane entries about food supplies, dig timetables and rotas, only the date that the professor was due to arrive at the site was marked out, with a bright red exclamation mark.

She stood back and looked at the desk, noting its carved legs, her eyes lingering thoughtfully over the battered drawers and shelves. It reminded her of a desk she played with as a child, in a rented house in Gibraltar where her father had been stationed for a few months. She and Arthur had spent many happy hours working out where the secret drawers were, using them as a hideaway for their favourite objects.

Suddenly Cate dropped to her knees and poked her head under the desk, using her fingers to search into the furthest corners. If she remembered rightly . . . She felt a small indentation the size of a ten-pence piece and pressed up hard. She heard a dull whirring noise behind and pulled her head back out just as a thin, vertical section of wood slid out from the right-hand leg. Trembling with excitement, Cate watched as a folded piece of paper fluttered to the floor.

She picked it up and opened it out carefully. It was yellowy, the colour of a faded coffee stain, and felt dry and flaky to her touch. The handwritten inscription was in Spanish and, from what Cate could decipher from the spindly copperplate, the map had been made in 1858 – not long after the site was first rediscovered.

'Wow,' she breathed, sitting back on her heels. 'How long has that been there?' She slotted it gently into her rucksack – it might not provide an answer to the mystery, but it was certainly worth closer examination.

Cate decided it was time to explore the site, but not in the daylight, not with tourists and backpackers wandering around. That was a job best done under cover of darkness.

Back in her room, Cate locked the door carefully behind her and began to unfold the old map on the floor. It was delicate work. The thin paper felt as if it would tear with the slightest movement, but finally she managed to get it fully open. It was only half a metre square, not large compared to today's standards, but it was neatly and professionally drawn.

Cate gently brushed a light layer of dust from the map and gazed at it, entranced. It was such a beautiful, evocative thing, the faded, hand-drawn ink strokes reminding her of stories of the golden age of exploration, when most of the world was yet to be discovered and determined men and women spent years in remote wildernesses seeking out flora and fauna and the marvels of nature.

Her first impression had been correct. It was, as far as she could see, a reproduction of the entire site of El Tajin, made well before the reconstruction had taken place.

Cate pored over it, frowning with concentration. She could see the distinctive rectangle of pyramids that had greeted her at the entrance to the site and, beyond that the vast, unmistakable shape of the Pyramid of the Niches. There were the ball courts and the remains of the other pyramids that stood close by.

To the north-east of this main group of buildings, the river gave Cate a clue as to where the hostel now stood, and from that she worked out the position of the dig. She tugged her ring off and placed it right on the spot.

It made sense that, if the team had found anything, it would have been close to where they had been digging and, using the ring as a focus, she began to scour that small area of the map, working methodically outwards, centimetre by centimetre. Sure enough, according to the map, the hut was in the middle of a whole host of ancient ruins, some of them stretching out into the rainforest. In fact, there had even been a building underneath the hostel where Cate was right now!

She grinned, half fascinated, half freaked by the thought that somewhere underneath her, in the thick tangle of roots and soil of the jungle, lay the remains of the vast town. Perhaps Cate was sitting above a house, or a temple, maybe even a site of sacrifice or a mass burial ground. It was pretty damn spooky.

Her knees aching on the bare wooden floor, she sat back and looked at the map from a distance. Something suddenly struck her. The squares and triangles obviously denoted buildings, she could recognise the meandering river, but what were the blue lines running seemingly at random from some buildings but not others? She looked at them again, puzzled. Did they denote the distance between important parts of the town, perhaps? Or maybe they were streets long vanished into the dust? There was no key to enlighten her, no way of knowing for sure.

Suddenly weary, Cate looked at her watch. It was only mid-afternoon, but she had been awake for hours. She carefully folded the map up and put it safely under the bed, took a banana from her backpack and ate it slowly while she thought. She had a quick wash at the tiny white basin in the corner of her room, pulled down the raffia blinds and crawled gratefully into bed.

Two hours later, she woke to the sound of her phone bleeping next to her ear.

'Marcus,' Cate said groggily. 'What's up?'

'That list you gave us – brilliant work from you and Arthur, by the way – but it came in just too late. Another site was hit this morning – four dead, more treasures gone. And we missed it.' He sounded despondent.

'I'm sorry, Marcus,' said Cate. She understood his frustration. No matter what they did, it seemed that the criminals were always one step ahead of them.

'There's more bad news. Novak Dabrowski,' Marcus said flatly. 'We know who he is, in fact we know him very well. But not as Novak Dabrowski – we called him Marek Bronicz. He worked on secondment for IMIA.'

He fell silent. Outside the wind was getting up, whipping around the hostel, rattling at the window. The overhanging trees were scratching on the roof just above her.

'He worked for you?' Cate whispered, not sure if she had heard right. 'He worked for IMIA?'

'Yes, Cate. For IMIA. For six months. In the Mediterranean sector, which is why Dave Osbourne never met him. Pity – he would have recognised him right away.'

'What happened?' Cate asked quietly. 'How on earth did Novak end up working for Johnny James in LA?'

'We quickly realised that he wasn't right for IMIA,' explained Marcus. 'He was just too violent, too unpredictable, and he was suspected of stealing gold bullion from a heist we intercepted in Sicily. It was the final straw and Henri got rid of him and refused to pass him on to another spy organisation. He must have gone private then, got a job with Johnny James.'

Cate thought back to those cold blue eyes in the pale face, staring at her intently outside Johnny James's office. She suddenly remembered and felt sick. She had been talking about her dad,

Graeme Carlisle. She had given Novak her name, handed him her identity on a plate. What an idiot she had been. She could kick herself.

'Bronicz was one of the back-up crew who helped to rescue you from *The Good Times*,' Marcus was saying. 'He would have known exactly who you were. He probably recognised you the first time he set eyes on you at Johnny James's house and, if he was up to anything criminal, he would have seen you as a danger, a direct threat. Until we find out otherwise, we have to assume he is the most likely candidate behind the attempts on your life. He must have had Gabriel in his pocket – he might even have been the second man in the truck.'

'When I saw him at the marina he was injured,' Cate said suddenly. 'He was limping and his arm was in a sling. When I defended Ritchie, I hit the assailant on his right arm. It must have been Novak in the truck. He must have followed me from Johnny James's place. I'm sure you're right Marcus – he was on to me the minute he saw me.'

There was a silence.

'It it's any consolation, those bugs you planted on Burt have paid off big time though,' Marcus said. 'He's been calling round all his old buddies, trying to find someone who can get him a false passport. Looks like he's about to do a runner, which means he's probably scared and ready to talk. We're picking him up this evening. In the meantime, try not to worry. Henri and I think that you're pretty safe where you are and we've an alert out for Dabrowski in LA and all airports and borders in and out of Mexico. But even so, I know I don't have to tell you to keep your head down and watch out.'

CHAPTER 17

'I forgot, someone was asking for you,' Maria said as she handed Cate a thick porcelain mug containing a wickedly strong-looking coffee at the end of an amazing meal. Maria had cooked spicy chilli fajitas followed by delicious churros – a sort of cross between a donut and a fritter, Cate thought. She was now sitting in a comfy chair underneath a large fan to enjoy her coffee and daydream about Michel.

'A man phoned,' Maria said. 'He didn't leave his name. Said he wasn't sure if you were here, but was just checking anyway.'

Cate stared back at Maria, all thoughts of an easy few hours gone and replaced by a wave of fear. Novak Dabrowski. It had to be him.

She could kick herself. Why on earth had she been stupid enough to sign in as Cate Carlisle? Marcus had offered her a false passport, arguing that it would be safer than using her own. She should have listened to him.

'How long ago did he call?' Cate tried to keep her voice calm.

'About two hours ago. When you were in your room. I told

him you'd be back later. That OK?'

Cate stood up quickly. She had to stay calm. 'Maria,' she said casually, 'I fancy a trip to town. To Paplanta. What time's the next bus out of here?'

Maria looked up at the plastic clock behind reception. 'It's gone. No more now till tomorrow.'

'Can you call me a taxi, Maria?'

The Mexican woman grinned. '*Te cae*. Are you serious? There is only one – and now it is siesta time. Maybe tonight?'

Cate thought fast. She had to get out of the hostel and find somewhere to hide until she could work out how to get safely back to Veracruz.

Her heart racing, Cate took the stairs up to the room two steps at a time. In seconds, her rucksack was packed, the precious spy gear zipped into an invisible interior pocket, but as Cate did a quick final check of the room she spotted the old map lying under her now-bare bed and grabbed it. She wasn't leaving that behind.

Downstairs, Maria was nowhere to be seen. She slipped quietly out of the door, around the back of the hostel and into the humid gloom of the jungle. She couldn't risk being out in the open now.

Staying close to the clearing, she pushed her way carefully through the vines that hung from the trees like curtains, steering clear of the strange-looking plants that grew all around. High above her, creatures chattered and grunted restlessly in the trees, watching her closely, wary but not yet alarmed. Ahead of her she saw the bright plumage and unmistakable oversized bill of a toucan meandering its way through the overgrowth. At any other time she would have been enthralled by this close-up of nature's most colourful beings, but now every strange movement and sudden sound made her heart skip a beat, pushed her breathing faster, her heart pounding with a savage fear.

Cate crossed the river, wider now than it was at the dig, jumping from stone to stone, holding her rucksack high above her head. The cool of the water provided a welcome relief from the humidity.

She stopped by the bank and tried to call Marcus, waving away the swarms of mosquitoes that buzzed around her head as she did. His phone went straight to voicemail so, in desperation, she texted him instead.

Novak on his way. Need to leave immediately. Pls send transport.

Eventually she was back at the dig, looking out from the jungle towards the hut. She sat down against a tree, pulled out her binoculars and made herself comfortable. For now, she was in no hurry to leave the safety of her jungle cover.

She looked down at her phone, hoping for a return message from Marcus. The signal was low here, and flickered in and out of range. She reached into a side pocket of her rucksack and pulled out the powerful hyper-dongle that Arthur had given to her and plugged it in. The signal picked up, but her inbox remained annoyingly quiet.

She hated to beg for help, but this time she had no choice. If Novak was determined enough to come all this way to find her, then he must really mean business.

It was hard to keep her imagination in check. After all, he could be close by even now, waiting for her, a gun in his hand, a bullet with her name on. She had never felt so lonely, so far away from home.

Behind her, a sudden shrill shriek had her leaping to her feet, but it was only a hunting eagle, rising up from a nearby tree before floating majestically out over the bright green treetops.

Night came suddenly. The darkness dropped like a blanket over the tops of the trees and the temperature plummeted with it. Cate stood up and eased out her stiff legs. These rainforests held wild cats, hunters like pumas and jaguars, not to mention the odd nasty reptile, and Cate knew that she was far more vulnerable to attack in the darkness. It was time to take shelter. Scanning the clearing and the jungle fringe one more time, she ran to the hut and went inside.

She stood for a minute or two, waiting for her heart to stop racing and her breathing to return to normal; then she set about securing her hideout. There was a door bolt, but nothing for it to go into, just splintered wood. Cate looked down. At her feet was a thin metal wedge, presumably used to keep the door open. She pushed it hard underneath the bottom of the door and then jammed a chair firmly under the handle. It would do for now.

She was cold, sore, and craved a hot drink. Using her torch she found a battered saucepan on the shelf and filled it with water from a bottle, switched on the electric ring and said a prayer of thanks as it glowed red.

Whilst she waited for the water to boil, she pulled the spy kit out of her bag and found the tin containing the night-vision lenses. Despite her anxiety, she felt a growing excitement as she put the lenses in.

She looked about her, blinking hard, then reached for the tiny remote control, pressing the green button firmly down. Instantly, the darkness lifted, the room was filled with colours so bright that it seemed as if sunlight was flooding in! Cate looked around her.

She tried the zoom-in option, and her close-up vision became sharper. She looked down at the floor and she could see every speck of dust, the tiny cracks in the floorboards, the grime between them.

'Wow,' said Cate, 'I'm an eagle.'

Cheered up, she switched on her torch again, removed the lenses and stored them carefully away. With her vision back to normal, she made a cup of tea, stashed her rucksack under Amber's bed and sat on the bare mattress, wide awake, waiting for first light.

To distract herself, Cate looked up at the pictures and slogans plastered on the slats of the bed above her as she sipped her drink. There were photographs of Gandhi, of Obama and Mandela, as well as famous explorers and anthropologists – Darwin, David Attenborough, and a fair-haired, white-bearded man called Thor Heyerdahl. Cate did a double-take. The name was familiar . . . and somewhere in the back of her mind she remembered her father telling her about the famous Norwegian explorer who had set out to prove that the Egyptians could have made it across the Atlantic to Peru.

She turned to the books on the side table and scrabbled through them until she found what she was looking for. *A Compendium of Great Twentieth Century Explorers.* She flicked through the pages until she came to Thor Heyerdahl. There he was, standing on the deck of what looked like a primitive sailing raft, his long blond hair flowing, a modern-day Viking.

A prolific explorer, Thor Heyerdahl had become convinced that Egyptians had made the epic voyage from Africa to South America, travelling by sea and then land, bringing with them their pyramid architecture, sun worship, and an obsession with astrology and calendars. Despite widespread derision from the scientific community, the Norwegian had been determined to prove his point. Using early African boat-building techniques, he had created a raft out of papyrus reeds, named her *Ra* after the Egyptian sun god, and set out from North Africa in 1969. *Ra* had broken apart, but he tried again the following year with *Ra II* and this time made it six thousand kilometres across the Atlantic, landing safely in Barbados in the Caribbean. Proof, he said, that the Egyptians could indeed have made it to South America.

There were other theories too. He believed that Vikings had settled on the East Coast of America; in Peru he had heard a legend that the Incas had told of white gods who had come from the north in the morning of time. They had white skins and long beards and were taller than the Incas. Heyerdahl had never stopped searching for proof that ancient people travelled further than experts had ever believed.

Cate scanned through the last few pages of the chapter. Despite making the voyage successfully, and selling thousands of books about his travels to an adoring public, most of Heyerdahl's theories were still dismissed as fantasy by his fellow scientists and he died in 2002 without ever being taken seriously.

Cate closed the book thoughtfully. Was Heyerdahl the Thor that Jade had been talking about on Twitter? And if so, what did her message mean? *Thor was so wrong and yet so right* – about what?

Cate gave up trying to work it out and looked at her watch. Nine hours to go till dawn. She would have to move on soon, it was dangerous to stay in one spot for too long.

Then she heard him – heavy footsteps on the hard earth outside the hut, walking slowly towards the door. She saw a face at the window, peering into the room. Terrified, she shrank back against the wall.

Her heart in her mouth, penknife in hand, Cate edged along the wall to the door and stood beside it, waiting for it to open. Surprise, if used wisely, was a valuable weapon. It was one of her mantras.

The person was at the door now, pushing against Cate's makeshift barricade. The timber strained and bent as he put his weight against it. Cate tightened her grip on her knife and readied herself for attack.

Suddenly the door burst open, the chair flew across the room, and Cate raised her arm to strike – then pulled back in surprise.

'Ritchie!' she cried, relief flooding her body as he fell into the room, banging his head on the low door frame as he did. 'What on earth are you doing here?'

He turned to her, rubbing his head ruefully. 'I could ask you the same question, Cate.'

'How did you know I was here?' Cate persisted. The relief that it had been Ritchie, not Novak Dabrowski, made her feel almost giddy.

'Nancy Kyle,' he said. 'You said you were with her in your text. And my uncle has her number.'

Cate mentally kicked herself for not being more careful. She'd forgotten how every celeb seemed to know each other – and that Nancy had even been at Johnny James's party.

'She was a bit cagey when I rang her,' Ritchie continued, 'but as soon as I explained who I was she couldn't have been more charming. She said she hadn't got a clue where you were and that you'd cleared off without telling anyone where you were going and your mum was furious. Apparently it had taken three head massages and a bottle of Moët to calm her down. Actually, they assumed that I was meeting you somewhere! But then Nancy remembered that, when you were having dinner, you had mentioned that you wanted to visit "some historical thingy" as she put it.

'There aren't that many sites close to Veracruz so I put two and two together. I rang a hostel – there aren't that many after all – and struck lucky with the first one I tried. The receptionist said you had checked in and I tried your cell, but the call just went to voicemail.

'When I got up here your room was empty – in fact the door wasn't locked and it seemed like you'd left, but the receptionist said you'd paid for a week. She said you'd talked about getting a lift to Paplanta, but she wasn't sure how you would find one.

'I went to the museum and the other hostels – I even checked on the site itself in case you were wandering around there. Finally I stumbled across this place. Amber said they were living in a remote hut, and so I reckoned this must be it – and of course I wanted to have a look. I should have guessed that you would have found this place before me!'

They sat down at the table and Ritchie produced some chocolate from one of the many zipped pockets on his khaki jacket and offered it to Cate. 'I think Maria thought I was a boyfriend, running after you to propose or something.'

Cate flushed. Michel was back in her life, but she was surprised at just how happy she was to see Ritchie.

'Don't worry,' Ritchie laughed, 'cute as you are, it wasn't exactly my idea to come here. It was my uncle's. He was worried about you and suggested I try to track you down. And when I worked out you were in El Tajin, well, that was the push I needed.' He looked sombre. 'I should have come down earlier, to look for the twins myself. I wanted to, but my uncle told me to leave it to the professionals.'

He smiled then. 'Cate, let's work on this together. I kinda think that we would make a good team. I'm beginning to realise that there's more to you than meets the eye. For instance, why did you leave Veracruz in such a mad rush after you'd only just got there?'

Cate looked at Ritchie thoughtfully. Usually she worked alone, trusting in her own wit, with Arthur and IMIA as a back-up. But it would be good to have a partner, especially one so reassuringly large and strong as Ritchie.

'Nancy convinced Mum and me to come with her and Lucas to Veracruz to keep her company,' she said finally. 'When I learned how close we were to El Tajin, I couldn't resist coming here to have a look for myself. It was a spur of the moment thing, really. I knew Mum wouldn't want me to, so I didn't tell her.'

She wasn't lying, but of course she couldn't – wouldn't – confide in him completely. Some things had to be kept secret. Including the fact that she had been sent here as a spy for IMIA.

'I thought I might be able to find clues that would help locate the twins,' she said. 'And here I am.'

'And have you found anything?' asked Ritchie eagerly.

'I've had a good look around the site, I've searched the hut, I've even gone through old maps and charts. Nothing. Maria the receptionist believes that the attackers didn't come or go by road, but I'm not sure how accurate that information is.' She sighed and took a bite of chocolate. 'Ritchie, can I ask you something, about your Uncle Jack?'

'Sure,' said Ritchie.

'Did you know that Amber and Jade weren't the only people he was sponsoring in Mexico? That he was also covering the costs of digs in about ten sites all over the country?'

Ritchie shrugged. 'No. But Uncle Jack has a huge charitable

179

foundation that funds hundreds of projects all over the world. He wouldn't tell me about all of them – no reason to. In any case, he probably loses track himself. Ned, his lawyer, deals with most of the details as far as I can see.' He grinned. 'My uncle has a short attention span.'

As she took another bite of chocolate, a vision came into her mind of the lawyer whispering something to Novak Dabrowski as he stood, like a soldier, guarding the entrance to Johnny James's panic room.

'Ritchie, have you ever been inside that panic room – the one in the basement close to his office?'

'Not for a while,' he said. 'We used to go in quite often. He keeps lots of valuables there – cool stuff from his art collection. He absolutely loves art, as you probably realised when you saw his house. But in the last six months or so, whenever I've asked he always seemed to put me off. I think that weird-looking guard made him beef-up his security – and that meant not allowing people in to see it.' He gave Cate an odd stare. 'What's that got to do with anything?'

'I'm not sure,' said Cate truthfully. 'Don't worry about it, Ritchie, I'm just thinking aloud.'

Ritchie stood up. 'How about we start searching properly tomorrow first light? As a team. Two pairs of eyes are better than one. In any case, the twins' mother isn't going to leave it to the Mexicans for much longer. She's talking about going public, launching an appeal for information, for money to fund a search. I don't think they'll be able to keep a lid on it for much longer.'

Cate suddenly felt a wave of despondency washing over her. 'Amber and Jade and the others have been missing for nearly a week. We should have come down earlier, shouldn't we? If they are alive, we have to hope they're being properly looked after, with food and water and shelter, otherwise they are going to be pretty close to . . .' She left the words unsaid.

'I've been thinking about that,' Ritchie said suddenly. 'If they had wanted them dead then they would have killed them on the site. There's still been no ransom request, but there must be a reason that they took them alive. And we have to hope that they still are.'

He put out a hand and pulled her to her feet. 'Come on. I'll walk you back to the hostel and you can get a good night's sleep. Things will feel a lot better in the morning.'

Cate stood up. 'I guess we may as well,' she said, feeling under the bunk for her rucksack. 'At least we won't have to use those horrible chemical loos.'

She tugged at the strap of her rucksack, but it stayed put. Cate got down on her knees and slipped her arm underneath and, catching hold of the bag, gave it a good yank – but it refused to budge.

'Dammit,' she grumbled. 'My rucksack is stuck on something. Ritchie, do you mind moving the bed a bit? I think you might find it a bit easier than I would.'

'No problem.' Ritchie was at her side instantly, his large arms tensing as he lifted the bunk bed up and away from the side of the wall.

Cate crouched down, shining her torch into the darkness, and instantly spotted the problem. The metal tag on the front of her rucksack had somehow got stuck under a loose floorboard and, as she twisted and pulled at the tag, the board lifted and came free, leaving Cate staring in amazement at a small metal cash box.

Over her shoulder she heard Ritchie draw in a breath. 'What the hell is that?'

Cate said nothing, but pulled the box out. It looked new,

hardly used and the lock was secure. She reached into her rucksack and retrieved the laser from her spy kit. She held the top against the lock.

'Where the heck did you get that?' Ritchie exclaimed. 'It looks like one of the laser wands plastic surgeons use to get rid of wrinkles.'

'Close,' said Cate, putting on her Raybans for protection and turning it on. 'Same principle, different uses. But don't ask where I got it. Now, just look away for a minute.'

There was a crackling, sizzling sound and the smell of burning. 'Done.'

She used her penknife to flick away the charred metal. Pulling the lid open, she tipped the contents carefully out on to the bed. There was a coloured stone and a small bronze dagger, slightly corroded but still unmistakable in its shape. Cate touched it reverently, running her fingers over the red stones on the narrow handle, feeling along the blunted blade.

'Incredible,' Ritchie breathed above her. 'Do you think it's for real?'

'I have no idea,' Cate said quietly. 'We need to get it to an expert. But what's this?'

She picked up a piece of folded white paper and stared down at it. It was a simple map, signed in Amber's flamboyant signature. Ritchie sat down on the bed and peered at it over her shoulder.

'There's us here,' Cate said, placing her finger on the crudely drawn hut. 'And . . . what's this?'

She pointed to a triangle, highlighted with a red asterisk, sited a kilometre or so north-east of the dig site, in the rainforest. On the east side of the triangle Amber had marked two green lines as intersections and behind it a blue splodge.

'Must be some sort of building. A ruin perhaps?' suggested Ritchie.

'Dunno,' said Cate, trying hard to contain her excitement. 'Let me try something.'

She pulled out the old map from her rucksack, unfolded it and looked at it alongside Amber's map.

'Bingo,' said Cate triumphantly. 'Look, this old map shows a pyramid in the same place that Amber has drawn her triangle.'

'Amazing!' said Ritchie admiringly. 'What are those green lines on Amber's pyramid, do you think?'

Cate stared down at the rough map, looking at the two green marks running parallel with each other, cutting into the centre of the pyramid. 'I think Amber found the entrance to a lost pyramid,' she said softly.

As they set off, the wind was blowing hard, wailing and moaning through the trees, and a light drizzle of rain fell across their faces. Above them, the howler monkeys were busy living up to their names and, faraway, Cate heard the sinister call of a coyote.

Despite Ritchie's burly frame striding beside her in the darkness, Cate felt uneasy, weighed down by a sense of foreboding she just couldn't shake.

Why? After all, this had been the breakthrough she had been longing for – and yet something felt wrong, so wrong that she had been all in favour of waiting till morning before they set out for the pyramid.

'We can go for help,' she had argued, as Ritchie had buttoned the map carefully into his coat pocket. 'Maybe we shouldn't do this alone.'

He grabbed her by the hand. 'Time's running out. There might be some clue to what happened in this pyramid place.'

Cate stared at his anxious eyes and nodded. 'OK, Ritchie, you win.'

They walked silently, concentrating on making a pathway through the jungle rather than conversation. It was hard going, with only the narrow beam of their torches to light their way. They had to push aside thick vines, duck and weave around overhanging branches, and try to avoid the meanest-looking plants in the undergrowth. Ritchie tripped, falling on his hands and cursing quietly as he pulled out sharp thorns from his palms.

Then, above the noise of the wind, they could hear the unmistakable sound of rushing water.

'It says there's water next to the pyramid,' said Ritchie consulting Amber's map. 'We must be nearly there.'

The pair looked at each other, the unspoken questions hanging between them. Would they find any sign of the twins?

The jungle began to thin out, the overhanging trees became less dense, the undergrowth easier to walk through.

'A path!' said Cate, playing her torch on the narrow strip that ran in front of them towards what looked like a low grassy mound. As they got nearer, they saw it was triangular in shape, thirty or so metres in width, and almost completely hidden by the jungle that had grown into and over the crumbling stonework.

'Awesome,' breathed Ritchie as they reached the base. He tugged away at large vines to reveal the stepped stonework and Cate ran the torch upwards. The pyramid was in very poor shape – it was barely identifiable as a pyramid.

'You OK?' said Ritchie, noticing her expression. 'It *is* kinda spooky, but you know it's only old stones. Nothing to worry about.'

'You're right.' Cate smiled at him gratefully and then sat down on a large chunk of stone. She shrugged her rucksack off over her shoulders.

'How did the police miss this place?' she asked Ritchie. 'I thought they had dogs searching for the students?'

'It's a big jungle,' said Ritchie, patting his pockets. 'They can't search everywhere, I guess. And unless you knew what you were looking for, it would be almost impossible to find. Sorry Cate, I'm going to have to go to the loo – I'll be a few minutes.'

Cate gazed round what remained of the pyramid as she waited for him, listening to the wind rocking the trees far above her. The place felt desolate, sad, unfriendly even, as if it didn't want her there. She shook her head. She mustn't let El Tajin get to her.

She retrieved the spy kit from her rucksack and slipped it into the inside pocket of her denim jacket. She had a feeling she was going to need it in the hours to come.

A soft bleep came from her pocket, a text from Arthur.

Daughter of Bright Moon owner played teenage vampire in last Johnny James movie. Her mum a big collector of Mexican artefacts. Does that help?

Cate took a deep breath and stared down at her phone. Every which way she turned in this investigation, there was one common link. Art lover, sponsor of ancient digs, who also owned the Erin, where Burt had done his deals and Gabriel had met his death. Just one name linked them all: Hollywood superstar, Johnny James.

CHAPTER 18

Rain began to fall, cold and persistent on her face, but Cate sat oblivious, staring into the dark, her mind trying to piece together the jigsaw puzzle. Was Johnny James the man behind it all?

It made sense. His generosity gave him the access he needed, the insider knowledge that was essential to organise these crimes. After all, if Johnny James was forking out all that money for people to go on a dig, surely it would be perfectly natural for him to ask them how the dig was going, what treasures they had unearthed, what precious artefacts had just seen the light of day. They weren't going to say no to a man who had been so generous.

And once he knew what was available, thugs were sent in to do his dirty work, with or without violence, as the mood took them. Maybe that was Novak's role? As an ex-agent he would be the perfect man to organise the robberies.

And Gabriel, where had he fitted in? Was he the transport man, who brought the treasures back over the border and left them at Mexicano Magic until things had calmed down, before they were then taken to Johnny James's panic room? And from there were they passed on to collectors, selected dealers, middle-men like the one she had seen on the *Ming Yue*, who could be relied upon to be discreet?

For a few seconds, Cate was convinced she had cracked the crime. But then she remembered she wasn't the only one who had come close to death at the hands of Gabriel. If it hadn't been for a good chunk of luck, Ritchie would have died that evening too on the Pacific Highway. And what uncle, particularly one who appeared to be as friendly and loving as Johnny James, would order the killing of his own nephew – the nephew he had given piggybacks to as boy – his own sister's child? But perhaps that had been a mistake by two thugs who failed to know just how much Johnny James cared for his nephew. He had certainly sounded upset when he left that message on her answerphone. But then, he was an actor . . .

The real question was why. *Why* would a world-famous film star risk everything in this way? For money? Surely he had enough money to keep him in art for ever. Or did he? Art was expensive, priceless even.

Cate imagined Henri speaking in his clipped way. 'Circumstantial evidence, Cate. All circumstantial. We have no real proof of his involvement. And until we do, we can't just arrest someone like Johnny James. If we were wrong, we'd never work again.'

As if on cue her phone vibrated with a message from Marcus. *Chopper due in 0400 @ Plaza del Arroryo.*

Cate nodded to herself. She knew where that was. The rectangular piece of land which lay in the middle of the four pyramids she had seen when she first arrived.

She thought for a minute then texted her reply to Marcus. *You need to get into Johnny James's panic room. It's the key to the whole thing.*

'I'm sorry about that.' Ritchie emerged from the jungle 'Ready to go on?' he asked, putting out his hand.

She looked up at Ritchie – decent, dependable, fun Ritchie – and a terrible chain of thoughts began to unravel in her mind. She was almost too scared to pursue them. Right from the moment he had bumped into her at LAX, Ritchie had been friendliness itself – almost too friendly. He had wanted them to keep in touch, pressed his number on to her. Then, when he spotted her at the Erin, he had insisted that she met Johnny James. Cate had believed it was because he genuinely liked her. But maybe she had been naive. If Johnny James was involved with the thefts and the murders, perhaps Ritchie was too. But then, he was almost killed on the highway . . . Unless that was a particularly elaborate set-up . . . Surely that couldn't be possible, could it? She tried to calm herself down. Working for IMIA was obviously getting to her – she had started to believe that nothing was as it seemed.

Cate's heart was pounding as she struggled to keep her expression neutral. She decided she could trust no one. Not even Ritchie.

'Don't look so worried,' said Ritchie with a smile, pulling her to her feet. 'I'll take care of you, I promise. Now, let's go find this entrance.'

With Cate crouching at ground level and Ritchie standing, the two of them worked their way along the north-east base of the pyramid, tapping, prodding, feeling for any opening or loose stone that might denote an entrance.

The wind had increased in strength and was howling so loudly that she and Ritchie had long since given up trying to talk. She glanced up at him as he clung crablike on to the wall above her, a determined look on his face as he tugged methodically at stone after stone.

Doubts began to creep into her mind. Had they come on a wild goose chase?

They had made it more than two-thirds of the way along the base when, without warning, Cate felt the left side of her body give way. Her hand, then her arm, then her shoulder fell through a hole that sloped down underground.

She let out an involuntary yell and struggled to pull herself back upright.

Ritchie was instantly by her side, pushing his arm down in the hole, shining a torch into the darkness.

'You're a genius!' He high-fived her enthusiastically, his torch waving in the air. 'Lead the way. You've earned it.'

'We shouldn't go together,' Cate said. 'It's too dangerous. I've read about these pyramids – they were often built with traps and shafts, and in any case the interior is probably unstable. One of us should go first to check it out and the other stay here to get help in case they don't come back. And, much as I hate to say it, you should be the one to go in there first.'

He gestured down at his muscular body. 'But you're about half the size of me. Less likely to get stuck.'

Cate looked at Ritchie, trying to work him out, to see if the answer to her fears lay somewhere in his face. Was he friend or foe?

He looked at her, his eyes wide and innocent, his face free of any tension, waiting for her to say something. She thought back to that nightmare journey on the highway, remembered how Ritchie had begged her to leave him so that she could save herself. Surely that was no set-up – Ritchie's life had been in danger.

But if she was wrong and Ritchie *was* involved in these vicious crimes . . . well, going into the tunnel and leaving him to guard what was probably the only exit could be disastrous.

She took a deep breath, made up her mind, and nodded in agreement. 'I'll go,' she said. She raised her hand in a gesture of farewell, then dropped to her knees, pushed the vines aside and crawled into the damp, dark tunnel.

After the noise of the wind, the silence in the tunnel seemed almost overwhelming. A narrow beam of light shone over her shoulder and Ritchie's voice came echoing down into the darkness. 'Good luck, Cate. Come back soon.'

Cate moved slowly forward, feeling through the fronds of reeds and weeds to the ground in front her, testing it with her hands before committing her whole body weight. The dampness was all-pervading, large blobs of water dripped constantly into her hair and on to her clothes, and the air was so full of moisture that every time Cate took a breath she felt as if she was swallowing a mouthful of water.

Something scuttled across the back of her legs, the torchlight picking out a small black shape disappearing ahead of her. Rats. Yuck. Better than snakes, but only just.

To her relief, the roof began to rise, enough for her to stand up carefully, pushing away the twisted roots that had grown down like a curtain into the tunnel from above. She felt a rush of cold air on her face and saw that she was moving into a wider passageway.

She reached into her inside pocket and brought out her spy kit, blinking rapidly as she slipped the lenses on to her eyeballs and activated them. Instantly the chamber was lit up, every crack in the rock, every stone of the floor crystal clear.

Cate looked around her in wonder. It wasn't a large space, less than six metres wide, maybe ten metres long, the walls and ceiling lined with flat stone, the floor covered in a dark red sand that felt soft and dry beneath her feet.

And then she saw them. On every wall and all over the ceiling – drawings: red, blue and black lines skilfully depicting cattle, human figures, children playing; the wide eyes an uncannily accurate representation of the native Mexicans.

Cate wandered slowly down the corridor, moving her gaze systematically from one wall to another, absorbing the beauty and artistry. She had seen cave paintings before in France, but those had been from prehistoric times, depicting hunting scenes, fires and animals; they had been basic sketches, little more than daubs of colour. These drawings were different: sophisticated storytelling, recording events as clearly as if they had been written down in a book. She was nearly at the end of the wall when she came across the battle scene. On one side, a group of native warriors prepared to fire a hail of arrows. Behind them, the distinctive outline of the pyramid of the three hundred and sixty-five niches showed that they were from El Tajin, defending their city against attack.

Facing them was the enemy, the prows of dozens of longboats floating on a vivid sea behind them. Cate looked, and then looked again, not quite able to believe what she was seeing.

This was no local battle for supremacy, no civil war of native against native, tribe against tribe. This enemy had narrow faces and metal helmets, flowing white hair and beards. They carried metal swords and spears and round shields. At one side, a giant of a man stood over all the others, resplendent in a flowing red cloak and horned helm. Vikings.

For a few seconds Cate thought she must be dreaming, although she knew, deep down, there could be no mistake. She had studied Viking history at school, knew that they had traded, fought and settled as far as North Africa, Russia, Turkey and even North America. But this – this was something else. These paintings showed that the Vikings had made it to Mexico!

Cate sat down on the ground, her mind in a whirl. What had Jade's Twitter said? *Thor was so wrong and yet so right.*

Thor had believed it was possible for early civilisations to make it across the treacherous Atlantic Ocean to Mexico. He had believed that the Egyptians had sailed across the Atlantic. But perhaps they hadn't been the only ones. Perhaps, a few thousand years later, the Vikings had come too.

Cate stared at the paintings. Was that it? Was this where Amber's map had been leading her all along – to wall paintings? It was a major find, but hardly fitted in with the heists of the ruins that had been going on. There had to be more to it than that.

She looked around. To her left the passageway came to an end, the wall smooth and unbroken. There was nowhere else to go.

She stepped back and took one last look at the paintings. Something was wrong, something disjointed. Then she spotted it. If you followed the trajectory of the arrows coming from the natives' bows, they weren't headed, as you would have expected, for the invading army. They were pointing up, almost out of the painting, to somewhere far beyond the battlefield.

Cate slowly turned her head, her eyes following the direction of the arrows and then, as if in a dream, walked towards the far end of the passageway. As she got closer, she saw that what she had mistaken for a shadow was, in fact, a gash in the wall – the beginning of a tunnel maybe, or a small cave. But a pile of boulders blocked the way – a recent fall, by the look of the freshly torn roots that had come down with them.

And then, sticking out from under one of the rocks she saw a wisp of black leather woven with coloured beads. Cate reached down and pulled it out, her eyes wide. A friendship bracelet. The twins loved them, she remembered. They always had a stack of them on each arm.

Cate put her hand inside her jacket and pulled out her spy kit, nerves making her fumble as she activated the heat-seeker. She began to move it slowly over the wall in front of her, listening intently to the slow, steady blip, hoping against hope for a change in sound that would denote that, somewhere behind that wall, something was alive.

And then suddenly the sound changed, swinging to a high-pitched shriek that echoed around the chamber. Someone, or something, was alive behind the wall. Cate's heart seemed to leap into her throat. She flung down the wand, pressing her hands against the wall, searching for something, anything, that would lead to an entrance.

She frowned. And then she had a brainwave. She reached into her pocket and turned off the night-vision lenses. The darkness was so overwhelming, so disorientating, that for a few seconds Cate felt as if she had gone blind. But then, as her eyes began to adjust, she saw the faintest pinprick of light shining above her, piercing through a pile of rock. Cate jumped up at the wall, her fingers clinging on tightly until she managed to haul herself level with the light.

It was a tiny opening, not much bigger than a fingernail, a damp patch just underneath it showing that it had been made by water erosion. Almost trembling with anticipation, Cate reactivated the lenses and put her right eye to the hole.

She saw them immediately. The four missing students were huddled together in the far corner of a small room, draped around one another, eyes shut, deadly still. Cate could pick out Amber and Jade, their distinctive dark curls lolling back against the stone wall. On one side of them, a blond-haired young man was leaning forward, his left hand resting protectively on the source of the light, a small torch that was flickering, clearly coming to the end of its battery life. On the other side sat a dark-haired man.

Cate drew back in shock, too frightened to shout. She thought about Ritchie waiting outside in the darkness, worried about her, and for a few seconds considered going back to get him. But she still didn't know for sure whether she could trust him, and she knew she needed to act now, that she couldn't leave the twins for a moment longer than necessary in their dreadful tomb. She grabbed the mini laser.

She reached above her to where she had seen the light, pointed the laser at the stone and flicked the switch, marvelling at the tiny sizzling sound, smelling the heat from the stone as the laser got to work. She scribed a small semi-circle, just large enough for her to wriggle though, but still it was hard work. Then at last, miraculously, the stone wobbled and Cate put down the laser gratefully and readied herself for the final effort.

She pushed at the stone, gently at first, and then harder as it began to move forward – and suddenly it was gone from her hands, dropping down into the chamber, where it landed with a quiet thud.

For a second there was nothing, and then a waft of hot, stale air hit her face. 'Amber? Jade?' she called. 'Is anyone there?'

Her heart sank as the silence swallowed up her voice. She tried again. 'It's me. Cate – Cate Carlisle. Please, can anyone hear me?'

She felt a wave of despondency wash over her and her eyes filled with tears. After all this, she was too late and four young people were dead because of it.

Then she heard a male voice, croaky – faint but alive. 'We're

194

here, we're all OK. Whoever you are, thank you.'

Cate felt her knees go weak and she clung to the wall for support. She swallowed hard, desperate to answer, too choked to talk.

Behind her she heard a grunting, shuffling noise as someone dragged themselves along the soft earth floor and a few seconds later Ritchie was in the passageway, standing up with obvious relief, brushing the dirt from his hands and knees. He shone his torch around, picking out the chamber, the drawings, and then finally Cate.

'Jeez, Cate,' he exclaimed. 'I was getting worried. Thank God you're OK. But what the heck are you doing here in the darkness? Put your torch on.'

Darkness? Cate was puzzled, then remembered she had her night-vision lenses in.

Ritchie played his torch around the chamber. 'And what is this place? Wow! Look at those paintings!'

He looked again at Cate and saw her face, and then within a few strides was at her side, shining his torch up at the hole, listening to the muffled cheers that were coming from the other side of the wall.

'You've found them! Oh my God, Cate. You're a legend.'

He flung himself against the wall, pushing his head through the hole. 'Amber, Jade – it's me, Ritchie. Please tell me you're OK.'

'Hey, Ritchie,' Cate heard Amber reply. She sounded frail and weak. 'Boy, am I glad to see you. Please, please, get us out of here.'

'Don't worry,' he said. 'Help is on its way. I rang my Uncle Jack.'

CHAPTER 19

Cate stared at him in horror. 'You did what?' she whispered, trying to keep the panic from her voice.

'I rang Uncle Jack.' Ritchie looked puzzled. 'He was really worried about me – and you, Cate. He's already sent Novak down to look for you. He said I was to follow you into the cave and not let you out of my sight.'

Cate closed her eyes. His men would be on their way now, catching a plane, maybe chartering a helicopter. How long did she have before they got here? A couple of hours, maybe three. Or would they just call some local thugs, get them to head for the site and find her before she had a chance to escape?

And what about Ritchie? Could he really know nothing of his uncle's crimes? Or was he bluffing, playing the innocent whilst leading the criminals right to her door.

Should she run now, get away from here, from Ritchie? But she couldn't just leave the students now they were so close to freedom.

'Hey, guys.' The voice coming from behind the rocks sounded

concerned. 'What's up? Talk to us. Please.'

Cate took off her rucksack and shoved it through the gap. 'Give me a leg up,' she said to Ritchie. 'I'm going in.'

Willing hands grabbed her as she wriggled through the hole, trying to ignore the sharp shards of rock that ripped through her jeans and cut her arms. Then she was in the chamber, seeing four pale, exhausted faces wreathed in smiles – and suddenly Jade was in her arms, her face wet with tears.

'We thought we'd be here for ever,' Jade sobbed.

'*You* did,' corrected Amber, her eyes shining as she kissed Cate for about the twentieth time. 'Mad, I know, but I never gave up hope. I have to say, though, I didn't have you on my list of potential rescuers, Cate.'

'Thor Jarson.' The blond man put out his hand and shook hers. His English carried only a trace of a Scandinavian accent. 'This is our sixth day here. We have some food and water,' he gestured behind him to a pile of bottles, 'but it was very worrying.'

The last of the four, a short, black-haired boy, was standing back, gazing at Cate with an anxious look on his face. 'I'm Stefan,' he said at last. 'Stefan Vilander. We didn't get lost down here. This rock fall was no accident. We have been the victims of a most dreadful crime. And all because of this.' He gestured around the chamber and then Cate saw why. The prow of a ship, elegant and slender, carved in the shape of a serpent, rose up proudly to the ceiling of the chamber.

The timbers of the boat were mostly rotted, but there was no mistaking the distinctive sweeping outlines, the deep hull, the oar holes still visible between the tar-plugged timbers. Around and within what remained of the boat were piles of helmets, green with age, steel swords, daggers and axes.

'A Viking longship,' she breathed. 'Unbelievable.'

'It's beautiful, no?' said Stefan, watching her closely.

Behind him, Ritchie was being pulled through the gap by Thor and Amber.

'Amazing. I agree,' Stefan continued. 'This longship will change how we see our past for ever. But because of this boat and the treasures in it, we were taken from our beds at gunpoint. Somehow these people found out we had discovered something important and made us bring them here.'

Cate forced her gaze away from the ship and looked at Stefan. His green eyes were blazing with anger, his thin face taut and rigid.

'How did you find all this?'

'Amber found the place by accident. We knew immediately what it was and how important, that it was a world-changing discovery. We were supposed to keep it quiet, to tell no one until our professor came, but somehow word got out.' He made a resigned gesture, his gaze flickering towards Jade. 'Then, on Tuesday night, men came for us. Four of them, armed with guns. They had explosives, sledge hammers, pickaxes. They made us get dressed, took our phones from us, and then forced us at gunpoint to show them the hidden chamber. The entrance was blocked so they simply stuck down some explosives and blasted their way through – they didn't care what damage they might do.'

The group fell silent now. Cate offered Stefan some water and he took it, his hands shaking as he put the bottle to his mouth.

She looked at Ritchie. 'We should be getting out of here,' Cate said. 'These guys need to see a doctor and we need to call the police.'

'They said they were going to kill us,' said Stefan, ignoring

Cate. 'They were going to take the treasure. Their boss already had a private collector waiting for it, somewhere in China, willing to pay millions of dollars for it. That Columbian, the one with those metal piercings in his chin, he was truly evil.'

Cate stared at him. Gabriel, it had to be Gabriel.

Stefan continued. 'The others were terrified of him. They did exactly what he said. And he was clearly following orders from someone else. He mentioned his boss a few times. Said how pleased he would be at this haul.'

Jade started crying, her sobs echoing around the chamber like an ancient wail. 'I really thought we were going to die down here.'

Ritchie put his arm around her, soothing her as if she was a child.

'So what happened? How come you're still here? Where are they now?' he asked nervously, as if he expected armed bandits to jump out at him from the shadows.

There.' Thor gestured to the wall of huge boulders, recently broken and mixed with red earth and roots. 'They worked for a few hours, taking things from the chamber, piling them up in the cave. Then they loaded everything up into boxes,' he explained. 'They were in a kind of frenzy. *Coins*, they kept saying. *Jewels*, *gold*. They were disgusting. Swearing, howling, laughing. Like a pack of baying animals falling on their prey. And then there was a rockfall.'

'The explosives they used must have disturbed the ground above us,' Stefan said. 'There was this huge rumble, the whole place shook. They were on one side of the wall, we were on the other and it all happened so quickly. Within seconds we were trapped here, buried alive.'

'We thought that after they'd gone they would at least tell someone where we were. We honestly couldn't believe that they would leave us here,' said Amber.

'But then, as the days passed, we realised,' said Jade between sobs. 'That they had just left us here to rot. All we could do was hope that people would come and look for us, woudn't give up on us.'

'Do you know who their boss is?' Ritchie turned to Stefan. 'Whoever it is must be truly evil. He must have known about the accident, that people were trapped. How could he leave them to die down here like this. It's inhuman.'

Cate stayed silent, watching Ritchie's face.

Stefan gave a wry smile. 'We had a long time to talk in here, to tell each other everything. We wondered who else could know about our discovery. Jade admitted that she was so excited that, when she was emailing her weekly round up of news to the twins' very generous sponsor, she just happened to mention that they may have found something amazing. And when he emailed back asking her to tell him what it was, well, Jade couldn't keep it a secret any longer. He was her sponsor and he had a right to know and she thought she could trust him. After all, he is one of the most famous men in the world.'

Cate watched Ritchie as he put his hand to the wall and leaned against it heavily. Horror, shame and pity was written all over his suddenly pale face. In that instant, Cate knew Ritchie was innocent. There was no way he could have faked that reaction.

'What are you saying?' he whispered.

'I'm sorry, Ritchie.' Amber was sobbing now. 'Really sorry. The only person who knew about the Viking ship and all the treasure, apart from us, was Johnny James. Your Uncle Jack.'

There was a silence. Then Ritchie turned to look at Cate, his eyes confused and frightened. 'You knew. That's why you were asking all those questions about Uncle Jack. Why didn't you tell me?'

Cate shook her head. 'I couldn't, Ritchie. I wasn't sure. Not until now. And if I had got it wrong, it would have been a terrible accusation to make.'

She looked at the faces around her. They were exhausted, which was hardly surprising, considering the nightmare that each of them had been through.

Cate had a sudden desperate urge to feel fresh air on her face, the wind in her hair, and to look up at the night sky. 'Look, guys,' she said, 'this can all wait. Please. Let's go. We know how unstable this place is – we don't want to get trapped again.'

But just then they heard a sound. Ritchie had suddenly frozen. He was leaning back against the wall, his head turned towards the open hole. He looked at Cate and she saw the fear in his eyes. 'They're coming.'

'What's wrong?' Stefan whispered. 'Who's coming?'

There was a silence. Cate looked at Ritchie, unable to bring herself to tell them what was happening.

'Friends of my uncle,' Ritchie said slowly, almost robotically. 'I told my uncle we had found a passageway. And he's sending people to find us.'

'Brilliant.' Stefan spoke into the darkness. 'We finally get rescued and now we are at risk of being killed all over again.'

For a few seconds Cate was almost paralysed with fear. She thought about what a terrible place this would be to die, down here in the darkness, breathing in stale air, seeing the fear in the faces of her friends, as they too faced their death. She shook herself. She couldn't – no, she wouldn't – let that happen.

'Come on,' she said sternly. 'We're not dead yet. We have to find a way out of this.'

She bent down and started picking up rocks. 'Here! Let's disguise this hole to the passageway with stones. It'll buy us a little time.'

Suddenly galvanised, the boys sprang into action. The three of them picked up pieces of rock, until slowly, painfully, the hole was filled once more.

'Now, switch the torches off,' Cate ordered. 'If they see light we're finished.'

Stefan was standing next to her. He smelled badly of sweat and fear. Cate wondered how soon it would be before she too was in such a state.

She was grateful for her night-vision lenses and wondered what it must be like for the others to be in total darkness.

Cate could hear voices now, getting louder, the sound slipping through the tiny cracks between the replaced stones. She put her hand into her rucksack and felt for the old map, unfolding it in front of her.

The men were very close. Cate could hear their footsteps, loud, aggressive, angry.

'The place is empty, Novak. They must have gone already.'

'Of course they haven't gone.' An Eastern European accent. 'They'll be in here somewhere. Hiding. Like rats in a drain. We just have to find them.'

'I thought we were here for treasure.' Another man, another accent – Californian this time. How many men had Novak brought with him? 'Not to hunt down a bunch of teenagers.'

'You do as you're told. We pay you enough,' said Novak menacingly. 'I'll find those kids, even if I have to blow the whole place to smithereens.'

Ritchie moved towards Cate, his hands held out in front of him like a blind man. 'This is all my fault,' he whispered. 'It's up to me to sort it out. Let me go out there, distract them, lead them away from here. They won't kill me – I'm Johnny James's nephew.'

Cate sighed and reached for his hand. 'They nearly killed you on the Pacific Highway. I don't think they'll care about you now, either.'

The voices were fading as the gang moved away from the wall.

Cate spread the map out on the floor. 'Thor,' she whispered, 'put your torch on. It's not that strong, we should be OK with it on. I want you all to see this.'

'What is it?' Stefan asked as the dull light flickered over the parchment.

'An old map of the entire site of El Tajin, dating back just a few years after it was rediscovered and before the renovation work started. I reckon we're in this pyramid here.' She stabbed her forefinger at the triangular shape. 'And here's the entrance that you found, Amber. Which means that right now, we're just about here.' Cate pointed at the blue lines. 'What do you think these are?' she asked no one in particular.

'Streets?' Thor guessed.

'I thought that,' said Cate, 'but it seems odd that some of the important pyramids don't have streets leading to them. That big one there for example – it has no blue lines near it, but this smaller one does.' She paused, running her hand along them, noticing how each blue line seemed to end up in one of the several rivers that bisected the site.

Next to her Thor let out a quiet yelp of excitement. 'It's showing the drainage system. It must be. At one point El Tajin held thousands of people. They would have had to build a water network and they were easily capable of building one underground. It makes sense. There are thermal springs in the jungle and they probably tapped into those.'

'That's it.' Amber was crouched down next to them, tracing a blue line that ran right through the centre of the pyramid. 'According to the map, a drainage channel runs straight under this chamber. Now all we have to do is find it.'

'Did any of you hear any running water?' Cate asked hopefully.

'No,' Stefan said apologetically. 'Not me. Anyone else?'

There was a dull thud and above them the roof shivered and shook.

'It's started,' Cate said quietly. 'They're going to blow this place apart.'

'Ritchie!' Novak's voice was muffled. 'Why are you hiding? Your uncle just wants to know that you're safe. He wants to help you. And your friend.' He paused then tried again. 'I'm not sure what Cate has been telling you, but I'm sure it's lies. She's a spy, Ritchie, a spy. She works for the bad guys. She snoops and she lies and she turns friend against friend. Go on, ask her. She's even turned you against your own uncle.'

'Don't!' Cate put her hand out to stop Ritchie as he began to scramble to his feet. 'Don't listen to them. You'll be sending us all to our deaths.'

He looked at her in the torchlight, his eyes narrowing. Finally he nodded. 'OK,' he said. 'I'm with you. Now come on, let's find this drain.'

'We looked,' Jade said despairingly. 'We spent ages searching this chamber from top to bottom for an escape route. If there's a drain we'd have found it.'

'We need a divine miracle. Or a water diviner.' Ritchie made an attempt at a smile.

Another dull thud rocked the room and a shower of dirt and small stones fell from the roof, rattling on to the Viking ship. A small boulder fell from the ceiling, narrowly missing Cate, where she was standing staring open-mouthed at Ritchie.

'Genius,' she said, reaching into her pocket. 'That's what you are. A genius.' She pulled out the heat-seeker.

'Thor.' She turned to the Norwegian. 'You said something about thermal springs? Just how warm was the water? Over thirty-six degrees by any chance? As warm as the human body?'

'Warmer,' said Thor. 'Sometimes up to seventy degrees. I've seen drawings of whole families in steaming baths.'

'Well let's just hope it's not further than three metres down,' said Cate to herself, switching on the wand and moving it methodically over the sandy floor as the roof creaked and groaned above them.

She moved urgently back and forth across the chamber, dodging the debris that was coming down in an almost-constant stream now from the walls and ceiling.

They felt another explosion and this time the loose stones they had put back into the wall began to wobble precariously. Any minute now they would fall and expose their hiding place to the men who wanted them dead. As she came up against Ritchie he whispered into her ear, his voice suspicious and confused.

'How can you see in the dark? And that thing in your hands – where did it come from? The same place you got your laser that I'm not meant to ask you about? Is Novak right, Cate? Are you some kind of spy?'

Suddenly the wand was bleeping a warning sound to show that it had found heat. Cate desperately hoped it wasn't so loud that Novak had heard it.

Cate paused for a second, hardly able to believe her ears, then all of them dropped to their hands and knees, smoothing away the layers of sand, scrabbling around to find a chink in the solid stone floor.

'It's here.' Ritchie grabbed Cate's hand and directed it to a narrow slit in the stone. 'Amber, Jade,' he whispered urgently. 'Over here, quickly. Hold the torches. Stefan, Thor, help me lift this slab up.'

They crouched down, straining with their fingers to try to release the slab from its bed.

'It's no good,' Thor panted. 'I can't get a grip. We need a lever.'

'Got anything in your kit?' Ritchie asked Cate with a wry smile.

Cate shook her head, looking around her frantically. The entire chamber was shaking now, the floor moving away from her as if it had been hit by an earthquake. They didn't have long. If they weren't discovered, they'd be buried by rock. They had minutes at best.

And then, she saw it. A Viking sword, two-handed, made of steel that would have felled a tree. She reached into the prow of the ship and pulled it out, marvelling at its weight, how it glistened in the torchlight.

'Sorry,' Cate found herself muttering as she rammed it underneath the slab. 'I know you're a thousand years old but, well, we need you.' She thrust her entire weight on to the handle, and felt the sword drop as the slab lifted slowly up before them.

Thor grabbed at the slab and lifted it away from the hole below.

'Oh my God,' said Amber, shining her torch into the darkness below. 'We've found the drain. And it's large enough for us to get down in it.'

'Let's go!' said Cate, relief washing over her. 'You first, Ritchie. You're the strongest. If anything's blocking our way you have the best chance of shifting it.'

He shook his head. 'No, Cate. I'll go last. I'll pull the slab down behind us. I want to see you all safely down there. It's my way of making amends.'

Behind them the loose rocks finally fell free, landing softly on the ground. The light from the torches carried by the gang flooded through into the chamber.

'For God's sake,' said Stefan, swinging himself down into the hole and putting a hand out to the twins. 'Come on! Leave these two to play heroes if they want. I'm getting out of here.'

'Go!' Ritchie urged, standing back, shielding the hole with his body.

Galvanised into action, they leaped into the tunnel, the twins first, followed by Stefan and Thor. Cate looked around for her rucksack, but couldn't see it among all the fallen rock. She gave up and followed the others.

Inside the tunnel, the steam rose up in great swathes to meet the cold air above. Cate placed one foot on either side of the water channel and began to move forwards. She glanced behind her. Thor was in the chamber now, urging her on.

'Hey, Ritchie . . .' She could hear Novak's voice, echoing down the tunnel, triumphant, cruel. 'You're not running away from your good friend Novak, are you? Your uncle sent me. He wants to talk to you.'

Cate and Thor looked at each other in horror.

'Ritchie!' Cate cried. 'Ritchie, come on.'

She tried to run back, but Thor stopped her. 'Go, Cate, go!' he said, pushing her forward as the sound of gunshots rang through the tunnel. 'Don't stop, don't look back, just run!'

And then Ritchie was levering himself into the tunnel as a huge roar came cascading down from the chamber above them and the whole world shook as if a gigantic bomb had exploded.

'Listen to the man, Cate,' said Ritchie. 'Run!'

* * *

The helicopter came swooping in at dawn, dropping neatly on to the vast grass rectangle that separated the four biggest pyramids of El Tajin, the down drafts from the rotor blades sending gusts of cool dawn air in through the gaping holes of the pyramid. It whipped through the tunnels and chambers and down to a small cave where the six students were huddled together for warmth, telling stories to keep their spirits up, as they waited for their rescuers to arrive.

Just before dawn, Thor and Stefan had volunteered to go back and check the damage, reporting that the pyramid was gone, flattened, almost unrecognisable from what it had been. Had Novak and his men been killed? It seemed probable. At the very least, surely they had been trapped and were injured. If Novak had left any guards outside the pyramid, they must have fled.

'The Viking ship,' said Amber sadly. 'Gone for ever. And we didn't even get a picture of it.'

'The find of the century.' Stefan was wringing his hands. 'The most incredible treasure trove in years and it's destroyed.'

'We saw it, Ambs,' Jade said, giving her twin a hug. 'Six of us – we saw it. It's not like poor Thor Heyerdahl with only his theories. Hopefully, the world will believe us. Perhaps something will eventually be salvaged from the ruins. And maybe, just maybe, there will be other Viking treasure nearby.'

But now their anger and frustration was forgotten, the relief of rescue sweeping everything else away. They cheered with joy at the sight of the helicopter and ran across the wet grass, leaping up into the belly of the chopper, desperate to get away from the place that had so nearly become their tomb.

'Hey, Cate.' Marcus was at the controls, his dark face wreathed with a huge grin as his co-pilot handed out blankets and cans of

Coke. 'I wasn't expecting a party.'

'Sorry, Marcus,' said Cate, buckling herself into her seat directly behind him. 'Lost my phone – I lost everything. I had no way of contacting you.' She gestured behind her. 'But at least the students are safe. Not that we can say the same for the bad guys.' She dropped her voice, mindful that Ritchie was sitting just a few seats away from her, the only glum face in the helicopter.

'It was Novak, you know, who did the heists. Helped by Gabriel. The evening before the students were kidnapped, they must have left their pick-up trucks in the jungle and hid out in the pyramids.'

'Yep, we know,' Marcus said, flicking the engine switch up. 'Late last night we raided Johnny James's house. His lawyer was outraged, of course, but shut up pretty fast when he realised that the Governor of California had signed the warrant.'

'Yeah, but what did you find?' Cate could hardly contain her excitement.

'You were right. The Mexican artefacts were there. Heaps of them. They were definitely on the missing list from the Mexican heists.'

Cate sat back in her chair. She felt almost giddy with relief.

'So that's the proof we needed?' she asked Marcus. 'That Johnny James was involved.'

The engines were revving now, the propeller beginning to turn above their heads.

'Pretty much,' Marcus said. He looked at his watch. 'If all has gone to plan, Mr James should be having a nice chat with Henri about now. Well done, Cate. Brilliant job – again.'

'But why on earth did Johnny James risk everything for this?' Cate said. 'It makes no sense at all.'

'Who knows?' said Marcus. 'He loved art – and although he

sold a lot of the stuff that was stolen, he kept plenty for himself. Maybe he just loved owning it. Perhaps it gave him a thrill? Or a feeling of power? I wonder if he'll ever tell us.'

The helicopter rose slowly up into the air. Cate looked out of the window down on to the ancient, mysterious site of El Tajin, at the pyramids, the pillars, the rivers, the ball courts and jungle that surrounded it. Despite everything that had happened, despite the lives that had been lost there, the terrors she had faced, she still hoped that one day she would return to enjoy the wonders around her without having to size everything up as a potential death trap. Be normal. Be a proper tourist. Maybe even with Michel.

EPILOGUE

There was a long silence and then the applause was deafening, the audience rising as one to clap the film that had just been shown on the massive screen that edged each corner of the vast Hollywood Bowl.

Simply entitled *Street Life*, and shown to a backdrop of Black Noir's soulful music, the film had pulled no punches in its depiction of the suffering of the many thousands of children abandoned on the city streets of Mexico.

The film had flitted from the drains and sewers, where the children slept on filthy rags, to their attempts to earn enough money to survive – begging at street corners, picking through rubbish dumps, pleading with drivers to allow them to wash the windscreens that they could hardly reach.

Some of the children were clearly struggling with physical disabilities, for others mental illness had taken hold, yet in the midst of the suffering, they looked out for each other, comforted and protected younger children, shared food and even money.

Cate brushed away tears from her eyes and glanced

surreptitiously along the row of seats to where Marcus and Henri were standing on either side of her mother, just down from Amber and Jade. If she didn't know better, she thought, she could have sworn she saw a tear in Henri's usually steely eyes.

Michel reached out for her hand and gave it a squeeze. 'You OK?' he asked anxiously. He had been so caring, so concerned about her since he arrived in LA just hours after Cate had returned from her debriefing in Veracruz.

Once she'd got over her surprise, Cate couldn't have been happier to see him. And, despite a few grumbles about their wasted girlie holiday, even her mum had welcomed Michel with open arms, inviting him to stay at her house.

On the flight back from Mexico, and despite Henri's pleas for silence, Cate had made up her mind. There could be no more lies, no more half-truths. If their relationship was to have a chance, Michel would have to know everything.

And this time he had listened, without getting angry, pulling her tightly into his arms when she had told him about the fear she had felt when she thought she was going to meet her death in the darkness of the chamber. He told her how brave she was, how clever.

'What will happen to Johnny James?' he'd asked her. They had been sitting on the beach at Santa Monica, cuddled close together on a rug and watching the silvery waves as they pulled back and forth on to the white sand.

Cate picked up a stone and flipped it around her fingers. 'He's denying everything,' she explained. 'Said he was used, that he knew nothing about it. Apparently Novak had access to his emails and knew exactly who he was sponsoring, and James said he sent Novak to El Tajin because he thought so little was being done by the authorities and he genuinely believed Novak was the man to find the twins. He's got the best lawyers in town working for him and he'll probably get away with it.'

'But what about Burt?' asked Michel. 'Couldn't he implicate James? Marcus spoke to him yesterday – I saw him at your mother's house.'

'Burt was just a bit-player.' Cate shrugged. 'He knew Gabriel from way back and let him use Mexicano Magic for storage. He didn't know what for and he didn't ask. But when he opened a crate by accident and discovered Gabriel was bringing in genuine artefacts, he was too greedy to report him. Thought he would help himself to a few objects.'

'His greed could have cost him his life,' said Michel thoughtfully.

'That's right.' Cate threw the stone towards the water. 'Gabriel must have been furious when he found out that Burt was selling his stuff on the side. That's why Burt was so frightened. He knew what Gabriel was capable of.'

A group of schoolgirls in shorts and T-shirts had pranced by like a posse of thoroughbred ponies, all long-limbed and glossy hair. One of them shot Michel a flirty glance. Cate gave him a sideways look and was gratified to find he hadn't even noticed them.

'My God, Cate,' he asked suddenly, 'does your mum know about Burt? That their shop was being used as the stop-off point for these treasures?'

Cate winced. 'She says she's never going to trust another man again. That they're all crooks, especially the American ones.'

'Mmm,' said Michel with grin. 'Wasn't she getting on very well with Dave Osbourne in the bar last night? He's American.'

Cate dissolved into laughter. 'I thought I was the only one who noticed.'

213

She grew serious again. 'Poor old Burt. He's been arrested for handling stolen goods and it looks like he could be up for manslaughter as well.'

'Manslaughter?' Michel stared at Cate. 'What on earth's that about?'

'He confessed to Marcus that he killed Gabriel. He overheard Gabriel talking to someone on the phone about what a threat I was to the operation. He spotted Gabriel later, near the Erin, and he guessed he was after me and tried to stand up for me. When Gabriel wouldn't back off, Burt lost his temper and hit him. He didn't mean to kill him – it was a complete accident. He panicked and left him there. It explains why he was so nervous that day, so edgy when we were in his car. And then when he got the text telling him that Gabriel was dead, well . . . no wonder he went so pale – and tried to do a runner. He must have been terrified.'

'In his way, Burt is a brave man,' said Michel seriously. 'I owe him. He saved your life.' He gave Cate a long kiss.

'And now, Cate, I have to ask you.' He stared at her intently. 'Your friend, Ritchie. Is he really just a friend?'

Cate looked at her feet, buried in the warm sand. She thought about Ritchie's face, etched with misery, as the helicopter had taken off from El Tajin.

'Poor Ritchie, he's completely distraught,' she said sadly. 'I got a text from him last night. He doesn't know who to believe any more. His uncle is swearing his innocence, yet Ritchie heard what Marcus said about him in the helicopter. He's no fool. He says he's going backpacking for a while to sort his head out. To Australia and New Zealand.' She gave Michel a quick grin. 'I told him about our romantic holiday in Snapper Bay.'

They smiled and Michel planted another kiss on her lips. Then he looked at his watch. 'Oh no!' He jumped to his feet, dragging Cate up with him. 'We have to go. The charity concert starts in less than two hours. Lucas is sending a limousine for seven.'

The applause died away as Lucas and Nancy took to the stage, the rock star's stark black jeans, hair and T-shirt contrasting sharply with the bright colours of Nancy's Gucci maxi-dress and her platinum-blond hair. She looked, thought Cate, like one of those macaws she had seen in Mexico, an exotic bird ready to take flight.

'Ladies and gentlemen,' said Lucas, 'thank you for coming and for giving so generously to such a great cause. I know that you have been moved by *Street Life*. Please don't forget those images and do anything you can to help those children – give money, lobby your politicians, write to the Mexican Embassy. Please, do it and keep on doing it.

'I have so many people to thank. My lovely girlfriend, Nancy Kyle, and all her fabulous fashion friends for putting on such an amazing show.'

The stadium erupted again as Nancy treated Lucas to a lingering kiss.

'And of course to my band – magic as always.'

He raised his hand to quell another cheer from the crowd.

'And I'd like to mention one more person. She's brave as a lion, sharp as a knife, she wants to save the world and sometimes I think she will.'

The crowd was silent now, listening intently to his every word.

'She's only sixteen, not much more than a kid, and I haven't known her for long. But she has shown me what bravery really is.'

Cate felt the blood drain from her face. She felt faint and clutched at Michel's hand for support. Surely Lucas couldn't mean her? He had wangled everything out of her, so knew all about what had happened in El Tajin. Please no, Cate thought. She would die of embarrassment if he mentioned her name. And then she'd kill him.

'I won't give you her full name, because she'll die of embarrassment,' said Lucas. 'And then she'd kill me.' The crowd laughed. 'So I've written a song for her instead. It's called "Just Cate" and this is the first time we've ever played it for an audience.'

A huge roar ran through the stadium as the keyboard player struck up the first few sweet, melodic chords. Then Lucas was playing a short guitar riff and the song was away. Soulful, funny, witty, the entire stadium was up on its feet dancing to the irresistible rhythm of the music.

Cate turned to Michel, then to Marcus, Henri and her mother. They were all smiling at her, huge proud smiles that made Cate want to burst with happiness.

'That's for you, Cate,' Lucas said, looking up at her seat as the final chords of the song faded away. 'You're one heck of a girl.'

ACKNOWLEDGEMENTS

Once again I owe so many people so many thank yous. To the fantastic team at Piccadilly – Brenda Gardner, Ruth Williams, Melissa Hyder and Andrea Reece for all their continued enthusiasm for Cate and her adventures.

To my terrific sons George, Conrad and Lucas who, as always, have been invaluable with their honest advice and creative ideas and most importantly, my amazing husband Graeme, who quite simply, keeps me writing! I couldn't have done any of this without you.

I have been lucky to receive such generous support from an amazing group of friends and family who have bought the books and spread the word.

Finally huge thanks go to the kind readers who have taken the time and trouble to review The Cate Carlisle Files and to all of you who keep coming back to read about her escapades. I'm thrilled that Cate is giving you so much fun!

The CATE CARLISLE Files

TRAPPED

ISLA WHITCROFT

School's out and sixteen-year-old Cate Carlisle lands a job on board a gorgeous yacht, moored in the south of France. She's working for the glamorous supermodel, actress and pop star Nancy Kyle!

But mysterious, terrifying events keep happening around her. Soon Cate's resourcefulness is the only thing keeping her, and the smuggled animals she discovers, from a terrifying fate.

An exciting, fast-paced thriller.

'Combining a glamorous setting with a fast-paced plot involving endangered animals, this is a great teen read.'
The Guardian

The CATE CARLISLE Files

DEEP WATER

ISLA WHITCROFT

When sixteen-year-old Cate Carlisle is made an offer she can't refuse, she drops everything to help a friend at an Australian marine sanctuary.

But there is trouble in paradise. A boy has mysteriously disappeared. Shadowy figures and strange lights haunt the ocean and hyper-aggressive sharks are wreaking havoc.

Cate needs her natural spy instincts, plus the help of her geek brother and glamorous friends, to save the animals and humans from an eco catastrophe.

'Light-hearted, highly entertaining escapism.
It will go down well with intelligent readers wanting light relief that is not dumbed down.'
Independent on Sunday

The **CATE CARLISLE** Files

www.catecarlisle.com

Go online to discover

☆ exclusive author interview

☆ competitions

☆ sneak peeks inside books

☆ fun activities and downloads

☆ and much more!